A VIDEOGAME STOLE MY SISTER

JUSTIN M. STONE

ELDER TREE PUBLISHING

Thank you for supporting my work.

Join my Newsletter

LUCAS

Lucas was so close to defeating the zombie king he could taste victory. After finishing the Race of Doom up the side of Mt. Lavahead, he had entered the zombie lair and fought his way through a horde of zombies to come to this point.

This was it. He was at the final boss and had all of the magical artifacts. Laying them out before him, he held up the Eye of Ra, the Feather of Zeus, and the Horn of Loki. Swiping his hand over them, he pressed X on the controller, and that was it. The whole room rumbled, or at least the videogame controllers did, and with the VR headset, it felt like it was really happening.

As large rocks tumbled around him, Lucas stared at the opening that appeared and the zombie king that walked out toward him.

What followed was a crazy fight. Lucas, as his paladin avatar, cast holy spells, and slashed left and right with his sword He put everything into this fight, attempting to take down the zombie king with his death stare and hordes of minions. But in the end, all it took was one good spell of holy water on his blade and the downward slice across the zombie king to finish him off. A quick cut scene followed, then loot sprayed out all over the place for the second play-through—gold, blasters, swords, and armor galore.

He did it! Lucas couldn't believe he had actually beaten the game and won the high score! And then, suddenly, his headset was yanked off, leaving him blinking in confusion at the dark room.

"Dufus, do you hear me?" His older sister, Madison, stood there staring at him, with his Virtual Reality (VR) headset in her hands. She was only a bit over a year older but always seemed to think she was his boss. She was petite, with long black hair that she often wore tied up in a ponytail.

"What?" he asked, then it hit him. "You... you can't go yanking away my headset! I just got the high score, I have to input my info, have to—"

"Mom has been screaming for you for the last ten minutes. Go."

"Lucas!" their mom's voice came from down the hall, as if to prove it wasn't made up.

He knew better than to ignore her, so he sighed and pointed at the television, where it displayed the less three-dimensional version of the screen. It still showed his high score, but now had a trophy image with a loading screen and letters that said, "Don't go anywhere!"

"This is a huge deal. Do you understand?"

She scoffed. "Go see what Mom needs."

"Madison, I'm serious. I've been trying to beat that boss since my birthday. Just... don't touch it, okay?"

Again, she scoffed, but at least this time she nodded. "Yeah, sure. Just... go already. She sounds frantic."

With her promise in hand, Lucas charged off to see what his mom needed. "Coming, Mom!"

He found her at her desk, pointing at the corner and looking horrified.

"Lucas!" she said. "Spider!"

It was a tiny little thing, but one of those scary ones with huge butts. He always wondered if that meant anything, like more poison or babies or something. Since he wasn't sure, he opted for grabbing a paper towel and cup, scooping the spider up, and depositing it out through the window. Inside a game, he could kill spiders all day long, but in the real world, he always felt a bit guilty.

"Thank you," his mom said, wiping her brow.

He eyed her with a frown. "Mom, how is it you're a grownup and I'm the one dealing with the spiders?"

She turned back to the work she was doing at her desk. "When you pay the rent, you can scream for others to help with spiders, too."

"That doesn't make any sense." He wanted to protest further, but as she was back at work, fingers clicking away at her keyboard, he let it go. Besides, he needed to get back to inputting his name for the high score win.

"I hope you didn't touch my game..." Lucas said as he walked back into the living room, but there was no sign of his sister. The image on the screen was both infuriating and confusing.

It was clear Madison had touched the game. The display wasn't even on the same screen. Instead, it showed an image of someone looking around wildly in a large cavern with racing cars on one side of it and strange, floating monsters overhead. The screen read, "Thank you for accepting your mission; please proceed to your briefing station."

Lucas frowned, glancing around. Not only had she touched something, it seemed she had royally messed up his game. The only reason he could think of for why it would be looking like that was if it were glitching.

She had broken it!

He sighed, picking up the headset and controllers.

"I'm going to eat all the marshmallows from your cereal!" he shouted, hoping she would hear him. It was that or break her phone, but he'd tried the phone thing last time and found that phones are unbelievably resilient these days.

Neither would matter, though, because just before putting the headset on, he saw the image on the screen looking at the window of one of those race cars, up close. In the reflection he saw Madison, staring at herself in horror.

Really confused now, Lucas put on the headset. He was there, with her, except he couldn't control anything. When she looked away from the car, he couldn't look back or make her step forward.

She was in control. Was this some sort of prank? He took the headset off, watching the TV image a moment longer, and shook his head. None of this made sense.

"Madison?" he called out. "You here?"

"She didn't go anywhere," his mom said, emerging from the room and smoothing out her purple dress. She smiled. "Thanks—for taking care of the spider."

"No problem. Where's she?"

"Madison?" His mom shrugged. "I'll make you two some grilled cheese with bacon, yeah? Maybe she's playing hide and seek. Go find her."

Lucas frowned. "We're not six, Mom." Still, he

looked, running around the house and calling for her. A sinking feeling took over, and turning back to the screen to see his sister's hands, gripping a steering wheel, he knew the answer.

The videogame had eaten his sister.

2

MADISON

Madison hadn't meant to enter her brother's videogame. In fact, she had meant to keep her promise. She had been turning away from the TV to go to the kitchen and grab an apple and a jar of peanut butter when the strange screen popped up.

It might not have seemed quite so odd if not for the man who seemed to be staring at her right through the screen. His mouth was moving as if talking to her, but no sound came out. She glanced around, then pointed at herself.

"Who, me?"

He nodded, his mouth moving as he clearly said, "Yes," though still the audio didn't come out. This was crazy—she wasn't even wearing the headset. Maybe the guy always did this? She still would have ignored him, except that she was fairly certain she had seen him on the cover of one of her dad's tech magazines. At least she thought it was him. Simon Borg, or something like that.

Curiosity winning out, she picked up the headset, eyes on the image on the screen of the guy waiting expectantly. She let out a nervous chuckle, then put it on.

As soon as the headset was on her head, the man said, "Oh, good, I assume you can hear me now?"

"Yes..."

"You did it!" The man grinned, holding a massive sword over his shoulders that hadn't been there a second ago. "And because you passed the test, we believe you are capable of joining us in the real battle against evil. Come, join me in my new world of creativity and excitement."

He held out the sword for her, and she stared at it, confused. So, it was all part of the game. Okay. Whatever. She was about to pull the headpiece off when she noticed something strange was happening.

First, the sword was sort of fizzling over to her, appearing in her hand, and a bright, bluish-green light was moving her way as well. It wouldn't have been so weird, she supposed, except that she could *feel* it. The sword in her hand, the light as if it were a warm breeze.

Weirdest of all was that when she put a hand to her headpiece... she couldn't feel it. All she felt was her head, and then the light surged before it all went black.

She blinked, able to hear her heartbeat, even feel the blood coursing through her limbs. Then the blackness faded, and she was standing there with a screen hovering in front of her and up to the left. A translucent screen that said, "Welcome," and included a window of stats. She wasn't very familiar with how all this worked, other than hearing Lucas talk about it. Sometimes she had looked at his screen out of curiosity, but her passion was books, not games.

What little exposure she'd had meant she understood STR meant strength, and DEF meant defense. Both were at one, which kind of annoyed her. Additionally, there were other stats that meant nothing to her, so she turned away from the screen. As she did so, she was surprised to see it vanish. When she looked back, the screen reappeared.

Looking away, it vanished again, and she took in her surroundings. Apparently, she was in a large cavern, a cave-type place but with openings above that led to daylight. In the cavern, she stood alone in a circular area of stone, as all sorts of oddities moved about her. Long-limbed, blue-skinned creatures marched along one wall with guns, while large creatures floated overhead, and others clung to the walls and moved slowly up or down. Some had pink, blubbery bodies with multiple appendages, while others were translucent and ghost-like. Along the base of the wall to her right were race cars.

It was all such a blur to her that she had to wonder if she was dreaming. How could it be possible she had been standing in the living room one second, here the next? And judging by the way she could feel each step, even taste the stale mountain air, she could easily rule out the idea of this being part of one of her brother's games.

She walked up to one of the race cars and looked at her reflection in the mirror. It was her, mostly. Though when she turned her head, she noticed pointy ears. Her hand went up and touched one, and she shuddered.

This was all too... crazy. Too illogical.

"Welcome," a voice said, causing her to startle and drop her sword. As it fell from her hand, it pixelated seemingly out of existence.

She turned to see a small, furry creature. Pastel green. It was round like a ball, but with large eyes, and reminded her of a stuffy she had as a child.

"I'm... sorry?" She glanced around, wondering if something else had spoken to her.

"If you're ready, we may begin the trial to ensure you're ready to meet Simon."

"Simon... *the* Simon?"

"That's right."

She scrunched her nose in thought. Maybe this was... it could possibly be... a test somehow? Some new tech that no one else knew about, but she was going to get to see firsthand? Or she had been shocked and was presently unconscious on the living room floor. The latter seemed more likely, but she figured that either way, going along couldn't hurt.

"Sure, how do I do that?"

The creature smiled, a mouth full of sharp teeth, but still the thing was kind of adorable. "Wonderful! Pick a car—any car—and I'll be your guide. You can call me whatever you want, but remember, I'll be sticking with you, and you can't change my name later."

"I... see." She shrugged. "Let's go with Easter, because you're kinda like an Easter egg."

Easter chuckled. "For now, but the name will do. Car?"

She shrugged, really not caring. Still, she noted that one of the cars was a yellow Beetle, and she had always thought Bumblebee from *Transformers* was kind of fun... even if she hadn't admitted it to anyone.

"This one."

"Excellent choice!" Easter hopped around to the passenger side and the door opened automatically for her. She entered and sat waiting as the driver door opened for Madison.

"Come on, Lucas," Easter said. "No dawdling. We should hit the road."

"Oh, that's not..." She was about to say she wasn't Lucas, but realized that might cause trouble. He had been the one to beat the game, after all. It was likely he was the one who was supposed to be pulled in here. Instead, she finished with, "...what I prefer to go by. Call me Madison, if you don't mind."

"Madison it is, then," Easter replied, smiling even wider if that was possible.

She entered, eyed the controls, and said, "What do I do?"

"Ever played *Mario Kart* or *Formula 1*? How about—"

"*Mario Kart*, sure. Of course."

"Then here you go."

At her words, a controller appeared in front of her, exactly like the one her brother used when playing *Mario Kart*. She had tried enough times to know which button was for gas and all that, so went for it.

Her car instantly shot forward. She released, and it slowed to a stop. "Where exactly?"

This time, Easter didn't have to reply, because a mini map appeared floating between her and the window, upper right corner of her vision.

"I see. Sure."

And then she was off, flying along the outer edge of the cavern, bursting out and turning around and around a ramp. Finally, she shot out into open air, screaming and shouting with excitement before landing on a road.

Here she stopped again, staring at the land surrounding her. Without a doubt, this was the strangest day of her life.

"When do I start the trial?" she asked.

"Oh, that's already begun," Easter replied. "Which reminds me, you should really... move."

She eyed her new friend with confusion, then saw the shadow appearing overhead. Her eyes shot up to see the massive fiery meteorite incoming, and she screamed as she pressed the button on her control for gas.

3

LUCAS

"**S**eriously, where is your sister?" Lucas's mom asked.

Lucas didn't know what to say. He was pretty sure he knew the answer but couldn't exactly tell his mom that her daughter had been swallowed up by a VR game.

It was the next part that worried him. When she held up her phone and said, "I just got done talking to Shayira, and she said she's been reading that kids have been vanishing over the last twenty-four hours. It's all over the news, too, and... Where is she?"

"I... I'll find out."

"Stay put." She held up her phone, dialing 9-1-1.

Meanwhile, Lucas ran to his room, opened up his

laptop, and brought up a chat window with his best bud, Jacob.

"Dude," Lucas said, "tell me you haven't beaten it yet. *Shadow Legends.*"

"I'm close, man, I mean... I'm at the last level and it's—"

"Don't play anymore without me, I'm coming over."

"What? Bro, it's dinner time almost. I need to beat this now if I'm going to have a shot before family dinner and—"

"Don't. Touch. It." Lucas took a deep breath, hoping his friend would listen. "This is serious, okay? I'll be there in five."

"You're lucky you're my boy."

"I know." Lucas signed off and bolted for the door. He wanted to tell his mom what he was up to, but knew she would never understand. No parent would ever believe their child went into a videogame, no matter how clearly that was the case.

Jacob only lived down the street, but the short run still gave Lucas time to think. He had beaten the game, and something must have come up to prompt Madison into the game, right? So were kids going voluntarily, or what? He would find out soon enough, at Jacob's house, he hoped.

Fear hit him as he slowed, though—what if she was

actually stuck in there? What if, by going in to rescue her, he would be stuck, also?

Generally, the idea of being stuck inside of a videogame sounded amazing. Getting to level up and fight baddies, to race and do all of the other fun stuff most eleven-year-old boys couldn't do in real life—that sounded amazing. But once he actually thought about it, especially when paired with the look of worry he had seen in his mother's eyes... that made him less certain. That made him want nothing more than to save his sister.

But maybe he could have a little fun along the way?

He was starting for the front door of Jacob's house when he heard "Pssst" from his left. He turned to see Jacob's head sticking out of the window, screen popped out, waving him over. The house, by all comparisons to Lucas's, was a castle. White roses outside of white walls, tall windows with a rosy glint to them, and a curved chimney that added a bit of fun to it all.

"What's thi—?"

"Shhh! Get over here."

Lucas jogged over, trying to not look so confused. "What's going on?"

"If you're coming in, you need to sneak in through here. My parents explicitly told me no visitors today. I'm kind of grounded for sneaking an extra chocolate bar from the stash above the fridge."

Lucas chuckled, making sure not to make fun of his buddy for his overly large tummy. He imagined sneaking chocolate wasn't a one-time occurrence.

"Wait, you're grounded but they let you play videogames?"

Jacob shook his head. "They don't know. So... hurry up."

Lucas's eyes went wide. His buddy was seriously risking his freedom, but not only on Lucas's account, at least. Since Madison was relying on him, Lucas steeled his nerves, climbed in through the window, and followed Jacob to his room

Halfway there, however, they were intercepted by Jacob's little brother, Ethan.

"Oh man, you are so busted," Ethan said, grinning mischievously.

"One hour of VR after we're done, if you don't say a word about this," Jacob promised.

The kid considered, then shook his head. "Not enough. Way I see it, you're dead if Mom finds out about this. That's worth a lot more than one hour of VR."

"Two."

"Deal." The kid laughed as if he had just won the lottery, then about-faced and walked away.

"Hard bargainer," Lucas noted with a nervous chuckle. Maybe he would have laughed at the situation if he weren't so worried about his sister.

"You're telling me," Jacob said, apparently not catching the sarcasm.

They continued into Jacob's room, where he had his VR setup with his computer. He eyed Lucas, then the headset, and folded his arms.

"Time to explain."

"Okay, but... you're not going to believe me."

Jacob's eyes went wide, "No way, you beat it and just came over to gloat, didn't you!"

"No." Lucas cringed. "Well, yes in that I did beat it. But no to gloating—now I need to beat it on yours."

"WHAT?!" Jacob put a hand over his mouth, glancing back at the door. So far, at least, no signs that anyone had heard him. He took that hand to point at Lucas. "No way. No way! I'm not letting you steal the thunder after all I've done to get here."

"It's for a good cause. To save my sister."

Jacob blinked, confused. "What?"

With a sigh, Lucas explained everything, including quickly finding some news sites online talking about missing kids.

"See, it's all right here," he continued. "And Madison went in. She's literally in the game!"

Jacob frowned, considering this, then scrunched his nose. "I don't know, that all seems kind of out there."

"Of course it does. It's ridiculous—but also true. I... think."

"You don't even know?"

Lucas threw his hands in the air. "How would I? All I know for sure is she was there, I had won, and when I came back she was gone. Maybe I've read too many books or seen too many movies, I don't know, but... it makes sense."

"Only to a true nerd." Jacob smiled. "Lucky you, I happen to be the bigger nerd of the two people standing here. So I'm in."

"You're in?"

"Yes, we'll do this together. I win the game, then let you try to go into it."

That was good enough. Lucas gestured for him to go ahead, then reclined on a beanbag chair with a can of lemonade from the mini fridge. It was time to watch his buddy try to beat the game.

4

MADISON

Madison continued to drive through the rain of fire and meteorites, screaming as she spun this way and that on the road. As another shadow appeared in front of her to indicate a meteorite's trajectory, she swerved off the road and went careening over the side.

She screamed, watching the ground come up first, and then Easter beside her shouted, "Roll! Roll!"

"WHAT?"

"With the controller, roll!"

She had no idea what her little friend was talking about, but took her controller and flipped it about all crazy like. As she did so, the car followed suit, so that she was flipped around and then landed on the ground with a thud, a bounce, and then they were moving again!

Her scream turned into laughter, and she had the window down, turning as she pointed at the meteorite that slammed into what was now clearly a bridge. It burst into flames and tore the bridge to pieces.

"In your face, asteroid!" she shouted.

"Actually, asteroid isn't accurate," Easter explained. "I'd say it's a meteorite, as once it enters the atmosphere—"

"Dude, don't care," she interrupted, then pumped her fist and let out a "Whoo!"

"I'm just saying..."

"And I'm saying, did you see us back there? That was crazy, that was..." She came to a stop, looking out at the land ahead. What was this place? Tall rocks with waterfalls, another of those large, floating creatures from inside the cavern, and what looked like a massive electric eel gliding along between clouds.

"Are you... okay?" Easter asked, staring at her with wide eyes.

"I'm going to die out here, aren't I?"

"What? No!" Easter shook as if trying to shake her head, but since she was basically one big fluff ball, it didn't work. "Come on, you beat the game! You deserve to be here."

Madison eyed her little friend, debating whether to

come clean. Ultimately, though, she decided that might cause more trouble, so she turned to the map and pointed at the green dot. "I need to go there?"

"That's right."

"And there will be more trouble along the way?"

Easter glanced back and said, "Speak of the devil..."

Sure enough, four large race cars were barreling down on her position, and one had massive horns on the front, its body painted dark red. Madison's eyes went wide and she pressed on the gas button, careening out of there.

The other race cars were catching up, and she muttered, "What do I do? What do I do?"

"Blasters. Use 'em."

"I'm sorry, what?"

"Blasters, of course." Easter eyed her controller. "Top right button, aiming with the right thumb. What sort of race car wouldn't have blasters? Oh, and oil to slick the road, flame throwers to burn oil. You name it."

Madeline couldn't believe her ears. She had never really understood the excitement of videogames, but now that she was in one and it was all becoming real for her? That first tap of the trigger button and watching as blaster shots tore into the tires of one of her pursuers made her feel more alive than she'd ever felt back in the real world. When the horned car charged up and she shot one of the horns off before slicking the road with oil, she was on top of the world. Fright mixed with excitement made for quite a good time.

"What now?" she asked, glancing around in confusion.

"Survive," Easter said, and started laughing. "This is so much fun!"

She looked at the little furball with a frown, but then joined in the laugh as she shook the controller to spin around, sending out blasts galore at her pursuers. In true button-mash fashion, she hit every button on there, sending out a barrage of missiles and grappling hooks, then shot out between the cars and waved at three other drivers who stared back at her with confusion written all over their faces. She shrugged, hit another button which sent those grappling hooks onto their wheels, then slammed on her brakes. The cars tore apart, tops skidding away from the wheels and then coming to a stop.

"You know, you're right," she said to Easter as she released the grappling hooks and pressed on the gas again. She turned to reorient herself on the map. "This is fun."

"I'm glad to hear it, because..." Lights flashed, and a disco ball appeared out of nowhere. "Congratulations, Lu—er, Madison. You just went to level two."

5

LUCAS

It took five attempts, but finally, Lucas jumped up and down with excitement as Jacob defeated the end-of-game boss. Jacob stood there in shock for a moment before whooping and punching the air. He turned to Lucas, removing the headpiece as the loading screen circled.

"Gotta hit the bathroom," Jacob said, starting to dance. "That took way too long."

"You might not want to. When I left the room and came back, my sister was gone."

That caused Jacob to frown, but he stayed put, eyeing the screen. "But you wouldn't do that to me... right?"

"I need to get my sister."

"Sure, sure. But... I mean, maybe I could get her?"

Lucas guffawed. "Dude, we both know I'm the better player, so—"

A man on the screen appeared, and immediately both boys lunged for the headset. Lucas got quick images of the guy and soundbites before the headset was wrestled away. With one controller in Lucas's hand, the other in Jacob's, green light flowed out and around them, screens appearing to float in their vision. Suddenly, both boys were being pulled in. The light changed to hit them like a digital shower, and they shared a look of excitement and terror before being whisked away.

The room was gone. In its place, the large cavern.

Lucas stood, already heading for the cars—as that's where he had seen his sister in the image on his TV screen.

Jacob scrambled to catch up. "Whoa, you weren't kidding?"

"I wasn't. We are literally in the game right now."

Even he had a hard time grasping how real it felt. He could feel the resistance of the ground under his feet, the wind on his cheek that blew in from the exits above. He wasn't impressed with the strange creatures —nothing that he hadn't seen in games like *Minecraft* and the like, though here it was all much more realistic.

"Welcome!" A small, furry creature came scrambling up as Lucas opened the door to a car that looked like the 1960s Batmobile.

"What are you?" Jacob asked the little guy.

It grinned wide and said, "I'm your guide to take you to the trials for—"

"No time," Lucas cut it off, already in the car and motioning for Jacob to hurry. "My sister's already out there, so..."

"Right."

Jacob ran around to the passenger side and got in, then frowned. "Wait, since when do you know how to drive?"

"It's a videogame, right?" Lucas held up his hands and, as expected, a controller appeared there. "Bam."

"Excuse me," the furball interjected, "but you'll be needing my help to—"

With a *vroom* of the car, Lucas peeled out, taking the Batmobile look-alike toward the nearest exit. He had seen his sister driving, so figured this was the first step at least. Since she was much less versed in games than he, she couldn't have gotten far.

"I just can't believe all of this," Jacob said, looking around through the see-through domes of the seats. "How do they make it so real?"

"I told you, we're actually in the game. This isn't a

joke, man, it pulled us in. Other kids are missing too. It's in the news. I showed you, remember?"

Jacob blew a raspberry, then did a doubletake at Lucas. "Wait, I mean, I heard you but figured it was your way of trying to do something cool without me. Oh, no—my mom's going to freak!"

Lucas blinked away the brightness as they exited onto a road that was missing large chunks in places. Smoke rose from below, though in the distance he could see green hills and waterfalls.

"So we'll make this fast, we'll—"

His attention was drawn to a flash of light next to him as that fluffy creature from before appeared next to him and screamed, "Dodge!"

"What?"

At that moment, a meteorite slammed into the front of the car and sent them flipping over through the air, smoke and flames around them. Jacob shouted and Lucas braced himself, as he considered their options. As he looked around, he noticed a screen appear in his upper left, and noted that it was flashing his three hearts next to three images of his face. Lives, he figured, and mouthed, "Oh, no..."

The car hit and exploded... and then he was back in the cavern with Jacob, eyeing each other as their screens showed two lives left.

"We're going to need to get more lives, fast," Lucas said.

"That, and..." Jacob nodded to the furball creature who stood grinning at them. "Maybe listen to this guy?"

Lucas sighed, but agreed, turning to their new friend and plastering a smile on his face. "Hello there, Mr...?"

"Whatever you'd like to call me."

"Fido!" Jacob said, and before Lucas had a chance to argue, the name appeared in blue above Fido's head. It hovered there a moment, then faded.

"Very good! Now, friend Jacob, let's get you a new car." Fido hopped over to the line. "I trust you're ready to listen to me and follow the map, this time?"

"Oh, a map?" Lucas wanted to smack himself. How many times in life had he learned that rushing in without asking questions—or reading instructions—could lead to pain down the road? Now he had one more time to try and learn from this. "Yes, please." Since he was already feeling quite sheepish, he gestured to Jacob. "Your turn."

Jacob grinned, selected a souped-up race car that looked like Jackson Storm from the *Cars 3* movie, if Jackson Storm had been amplified by a thousand.

"Right there, baby," Jacob said. "We'll take Jackson Stormageddon."

"Wonderful choice!" Fido noted, and the doors opened.

Jacob went to the driver's side, smiling like a child in a—well, in a videogame that just gave him the most awesome racing car ever, and climbed in. Sharing a look of excitement as the map popped up, they were ready this time.

6

MADISON

Madison pulled up to the crest of a hill where the road went between two mountains. A valley opened up in front of her. She paused, finally taking a moment to look at her level-up screen. Sure enough, it said that she was level two. That included strength and defense each getting a couple of points increase, and her other stats as well. One that stuck out to her most was an area that read, "Skill Points," of which she had two.

"What's that do?" she asked her new furry friend.

"You can use those to learn special techniques with the sword or other weapons," Easter replied. "Spells later if you get to that level, and even upgrade your car or... me."

"Or you?" Madison was curious, not exactly the type

to care about how this stuff should be used. "Great—I want to use both on you."

Easter's eyes widened. "You're... sure?"

"I am. Do it."

For a split second, Madison wondered if she had made a mistake, considering the way Easter was staring at her like she was an alien. But then Easter said, "Thank you, thank you, thank you!" and started glowing. The first point went away, and the glow intensified, and a screen appeared above her head that read:

Choose Form:
Cat, Dog, Rabbit, Lizard, Bird

"Wait, in books sometimes people have familiars," Madison said, thinking about witches and wizards. "So you'll be kinda like that, huh? A special animal bonded to me?"

Easter simply shook, muttering, "Choose quickly, but wisely."

"I see. Sure." Madison reached up to touch the selection, but her hand went right through it. "Ah, how about... Well, Rapunzel had a lizard, so why not one of those?"

"Why not, indeed." Easter seemed very humored by her logic, but as Madison watched, Easter transformed into the shape of a lizard! Still furry in that pastel green, but with a lizard shape. It only occurred to Madison then that the lizard in the movie had been a chameleon, while Easter looked more like an iguana, but close enough.

Easter sat up and stretched, looking like a nice version of that bad guy from *Monsters, Inc.* Madison liked her choice.

"Maybe that second point should go to your sword?" Easter said, though she looked very appreciative. "You've already done so much for me and—"

"Use the second point," Madison insisted.

Instantly, Easter glowed again, and this time she grew some very cool spikes and horns. The only downside Madison could see was that Easter had to watch how she sat so her spikes didn't tear the seat.

"Now I imagine I'll be quite useful in a fight," the furry lizard said with a laugh. "Thank you."

"Hey, what are friends for."

"You... you're my friend?"

Madison glanced over. "I hope so. For as long as I'm here, anyway. Speaking of the sword from before—"

"Oh, don't summon it in here!" Easter said, leading Madison to realize she could likely make the sword appear by wishing it so. *Awesome.*

"Why not?" Madison asked.

"That would be dangerous for both of us and the car, but especially me."

"I still have it though?" Madison wanted to ensure her idea of being able to summon it was true.

"You do," Easter replied. "When you get into a non-vehicle fight, just reach out and wish for it—and bam! In your hand."

Madison liked the sound of that. Dismissing the screen, she looked at the valley. "What've we got here?"

"The valley of the undead, with Simon on the other side... there." Easter indicated the map, then zoomed in on it so they could see what looked like a building.

"Great. Wonderful. What are 'undead,' exactly?"

Easter chuckled, then looked at her with unease. "You... really don't know?"

"I don't."

"But you beat the game, you... oh." Easter looked at her with skepticism. "It wasn't you, was it?"

Madison grimaced and shook her head.

"You upgraded me before yourself, so... I have to like you." Easter sighed. "But this is dangerous."

"It's just a game."

Easter slowly shook her head—she could do that, now that she had a neck. "It's not, Madison. You have three lives to start with, yes. So it's not as real as reality, yet. But you're in it now, and if you lost those three lives..."

"You're saying, what, I'd die?"

"Unless you get more lives along the way, which is potentially possible... Then yes. Dead. For real dead."

"No way." Madison scoffed. "You're making that up."

"I'm really not."

Madison eyed her friend uneasily, mind going back to her mom and how worried she would be if this was remotely true. At least Lucas was back there with her. She needed someone, what with their dad gone, having never returned from one of his work trips. It had hurt them all, but their mom worst of all. She had demanded answers, but in the end, the company and police all told her the same—that sometimes spouses leave.

Madison still wasn't sure she wanted to accept it, but with the way her friends had abandoned her at school, she was starting to understand. Sometimes, no matter how perfect you think something is, things go wrong. People change. The fact that it sucks doesn't make it any less true.

"And if I wanted to log out right now?" Madison asked.

Easter shook her head again.

"Fine, you know what? Fine!" Madison pressed the gas button, moving down into the valley. "I'm having fun anyway, though I hate to admit it. Let's amp up the crazy, see how much more fun it can get!"

"That's the spirit!" Easter replied, but before they crested the hill, Madison saw another car approaching fast from the rear. It looked like some sort of souped-up version of one of those race cars from the Pixar movies, but with way more weapons, fins, and all sorts of upgrades that she didn't understand.

With undead enemies ahead—whatever those were —and more racer enemies at the rear, she smiled at herself in the rearview mirror and mentally prepared herself for the fight to come.

7

LUCAS

Lucas and Jacob had been going through a tough time trying to reach this point, what with all the car chases and blasters going off. The best part had been when Lucas realized he could take control of the weapons while Jacob drove, so that they cleared the last line of monster-truck baddies relatively quickly compared with the first two waves. One of the monster trucks had gotten dangerously close, its hood opening up to reveal sharp teeth and a nasty, massive tongue.

Never again would Lucas see monster trucks the same way.

Ahead of them, they had spotted a car that looked like it might be a yellow Volkswagen Beetle, or something similar to the first version of Bumblebee in the *Transformer* movies.

"If that car shoots at us, take it out," Jacob said. "It doesn't look as intimidating, but who knows..."

"On it," Lucas said, ready with the weapons controls.

"I should warn you," Fido said as they started down into the valley where the yellow car had gone, "we're entering the Valley of the Undead."

"Yes!" Jacob said, pumping his fist and hitting the roof. "Ouch, didn't mean to do that."

"Right, um, why is that a good thing?" Fido asked.

"This boy right here *loves* him some undead," Lucas explained. "Get him in a convention with a room full of zombies or vampires, same as putting me in a... well, a reality game like this. Or maybe with a buffet of nachos and root beer. I mean those nachos with pump cheese, but also some plates with carne asada and jalapenos, or—"

"We get it, you like nachos," Jacob cut in, laughing. He turned to Fido. "Are there going to be zombies?"

"See for yourselves," Fido replied, looking rather disturbed at their attitude toward the situation.

"What do you mean?" Jacob asked, eyes on the road.

Lucas wasn't driving, though, so was able to see the surrounding hills and valleys as they drove. He watched with amazement as creatures appeared with red eyes and green skin. Some were more rotted than others, and all were starting toward them.

"Incoming," Lucas said and manned the blasters, already starting to tear into them.

Jacob let out a long, "Ahhh!" now that he had glanced at the zombie horde.

Out of the horde appeared a metallic beast that resembled a cheetah, with eyes that glowed red.

"What's the animal thing?" Lucas asked.

"Their herder, like a shepherd," Fido explained. "Only way to keep them under some sort of control."

"Who would need to control them?"

"Simon, of course. This is all part of the trial as far as you're concerned, but it's a very real world otherwise. Once you've passed the trial, you'll see."

Lucas and Jacob shared a look of concern, then Lucas asked, "Do I shoot the robots, too?"

"You probably want to try, as doing so will confuse the zombies. Excellent questions, Lucas."

Lucas beamed and started blasting away at the zombies and robots alike. As he did, though, Jacob grabbed his shoulder.

"What?" Lucas protested. "I'm kind of in the middle of something."

"Dude!"

As Lucas continued to shoot, he noticed his level go

up to two, but didn't get a chance to check it out as Jacob kept pulling on him.

He turned and shouted, "What?!"

Lucas finally looked and saw that Jacob was pointing ahead. The yellow car had swerved sideways as it was being overrun by zombies. The horde was coming in from all directions to such an extent that there seemed to be no way past them aside from something drastic.

"Go around?" Jacob asked with a shrug.

"You can't be serious."

"I mean, we don't know that person—and it's just a game, right?" Jacob started to swerve to try and drive around the horde. "They take the attack for the team, while we make our escape."

"Except, I keep trying to stress this is not a game," Fido noted with a bit of grumpy in his voice.

"And that's not just any random player," Lucas noted, staring in awe as the figure emerged from the car, accompanied by a strange lizard creature. The lizard was slicing around at the zombies, attacking like a crazed dog, while the girl summoned a huge sword and started hacking and slashing at the enemy.

It was his sister, and at the same time, he couldn't understand that idea at all. Madison didn't play games, and she certainly didn't know how to use a sword. This girl was kind of awesome, while Madison had always seemed sort of... less so.

"Dude, is that your sister?"

"That's... my sister."

Jacob immediately swerved back on track, shouting, "Blast those fools!"

Lucas was happy to oblige, sending blast after blast at the zombies and watching them drop. It wasn't enough, though, and the shots that hit the robot animals didn't seem to do much damage.

"Fido," Jacob called over his shoulder. "We have any more of those rockets?"

"They're on a recharge basis, so yes, you just have to—"

A barrage of shots went flying into the horde, followed by a rocket. "Figured it out."

"Apparently you did," Fido grumbled.

Meanwhile, the rocket went careening right into a large group of zombies and exploded on the head of a metal rat the size of a dog. Bits of metal went flying, zombies scattered... and a whole group of them seemed to suddenly lose focus, even attacking each other.

"Nice!" Lucas said, high-fiving his buddy. Both returned their focus to the controls as they rode in to meet up with his sister.

8

MADISON

Madison staggered back and reached out to put a hand against her car, a ringing in her ears from the rocket that had nearly killed her. Some idiot was clearly trying to help her but had shot it too close. She realized she had dropped her sword so reached out and willed it to come to her again, which it did.

She loved the feel of the sword. Although she rarely told anyone, she actually had a Japanese kendo sword in her bedroom, and sometimes practiced with it. Her teachers were online videos, nothing real, but it was one of her most calming, favorite things to do. Of course, that had nothing on using this long, monstrous sword to cut through zombies. If ever she had found her Zen happy place, this was it—slaying monsters in some imaginary world.

Never in her wildest dreams would she have thought that would ever be the case.

"Get up!" Easter shouted, leaping over her to land on a zombie and push it back, then land and sweep out the legs of another to trip it. "They aren't stopping, so neither can you!"

Madison grinned, stood, and got back into it.

Meanwhile, the souped-up race car was incoming, and as she thrust sideways to take down two zombies, she couldn't believe what she saw—Lucas and his dorky friend Jacob were in the car!

"I know them," she told Easter, then practiced a downward, diagonal slice. "The one in the passenger seat is my brother."

"Ah, in that case, I have an idea," Easter said. "Self-destruct."

"You want to self-destruct? I forbid it!"

"Not me. The car."

Madison swiped again and again, a bar on her screen flashing and showing experience points, or XP, rising like crazy with each kill. Her next strike brought her to level three as she said, "Not my Beetle!"

"You could alternatively keep doing this..." Easter pulled back as she swung her sword again. "Through... all of those zombies."

The lizard thing had a point. From what she could tell, it was a forest of never-ending zombies. As three would fall, twenty more would take their place. And as much as the sword didn't weigh much—only enough for proper balance and to tell where it was so she didn't accidentally cut her foot off—she was starting to feel the exhaustion.

At least as she cut through more and more, enough to hit level four, she felt rejuvenated and figured that's what STA meant—stamina.

"Fine! Do it!"

"Good choice, but..." Easter tripped another zombie. "We'll need to ensure we're in that car, driving away fast when it happens."

"Copy that." She chuckled, humored by the fact that she was even starting to talk like the nerds did when playing their shooter games.

Wait, was she becoming one of them? A nerd? She sliced off three heads at once and let out a howl. No, not a chance. A nerd couldn't do that.

Then, as Easter said the countdown had begun, the two of them started fighting their way over to the incoming car. But by then, it was close, barreling through zombies and directing its shots at the robot animals.

With each hack, she thought of the math test she had been studying so hard for, with each slash remembering the one she kept getting wrong and simply couldn't understand. As she cut a path to her brother, she remembered how at school yesterday some kid had put cake in her hair, and she had run off to hide in the bathroom. Where had her friends been, then? Why hadn't they come to her rescue? The thoughts gave her extra energy and she let out a roar as she leaped up and came down hard with her blade. Hard enough to send a shock wave out, knocking back the closest twenty or so zombies.

One of the robot animals faced her, growling. It reminded her of a hyena, but with angular metal and spikes. This one's eyes were dark red, almost sickly looking. When it charged her, she was happy to slam her blade into its open mouth and then twist, tearing it in two.

The robot fell, lights going out. As it faded, so too did the collective actions of the group of zombies between her and the spot where her brother's car had stopped. There had been too many, but now that they weren't all pressing against it, the car pushed through again.

Finally, the passenger-side door opened and there was Lucas, waving for her.

"Come on, get in, get in!"

"How long?" Madison asked her lizard friend.

"I'd say about ten seconds at most." Easter cocked her head. "Nine."

"Got it!" She sprinted, charging for the car, and said, "Back inside! Get ready to go!"

"Seven," Easter continued counting.

"Cut it out," Madison said, letting her sword vanish as she slid into the car, going for the rear side, and then pulling Easter with her. "Go, go, go!"

Jacob didn't need to be told twice, but as he shot off, she had to lean forward and grab the controller, thrusting it hard to the right.

"Not toward the car!" she explained. "Away from it —fast!"

"Two..." Easter said.

"Ahhh!" Madison shouted, covering her ears.

"Oh, man." Lucas saw what she was doing and did the same, while Jacob drove away from the car as fast as he could.

Ka-BOOM!

The explosion rocked the ground, sending zombies and robots flying all over.

"Next stop," Easter said, "Somewhere other than here!"

Madison laughed, turning around in the car to see the chaos they had left in their wake. The ground had a massive hole in it, bits of her yellow car still flaming, and all manner of incapacitated zombies littering the landscape.

When she turned back to watch them driving past more groups of zombies but ultimately leaving them behind in favor of the square, unassuming building ahead, she knew they had made it.

"That was the trial," she said, nodding to herself. "It wasn't so bad."

"Where'd you get that awesome sword?" Jacob asked, glancing back excitedly.

"First, what—what are you doing here?" she asked them. "Or better yet, what are we *all* doing here? This is insane!"

"We came to rescue you," Lucas explained. "I'm guessing that means getting to this Simon guy, huh?"

She laughed. "More like I rescued you. If not for me and Easter here blowing up our car, you'd be in some real trouble right about now."

"Wait, you did that on purpose?" Lucas asked, turning in his seat to stare at her, slack jawed. "Wh— who are you?"

She laughed. "Actually, I did notice these." She indicated her pointy ears. "I figure it's part of the game-not-game, but... other than that, all me."

"No way. My sister doesn't blow up cars, and she certainly doesn't fight zombies with a humongous sword."

"What can I say?" She chuckled, running a hand along Easter's neck, which the creature seemed to enjoy. "This place is bringing out a different side of me."

"And here you were thinking we had to save her," Jacob said, nudging Lucas.

"Ah, that's sweet though," Madison admitted. "My little brother and his nerd friend came to rescue little ol' me."

"Mock us all you want, but you're in it, now." Jacob gave her a spread-finger greeting—between middle and ring finger—that she recognized from *Star Trek*, but only because their dad used to do that. "Welcome to the nerd side."

"Please." She shook her head, not buying it, but then looked down at her clothes, straight out of a renaissance fair. Then the strange, furry lizard thing, that actually kind of reminded her of the dragon from *The Neverending Story*. Oh, no... she *was* turning into a nerd.

But maybe... maybe that was okay? She looked back again, the zombies fading in the distance. Staring at them and remembering the thrill of the fight, she couldn't honestly remember ever having more fun.

And as one of the cool kids, hadn't her friends betrayed her? She had to admit there was something about just letting go, maybe "being herself," that worked way better than all that fake stuff. Maybe she had found her calling after all.

She leaned back, actually feeling relieved to see her brother. They hadn't spent time together since... well, she couldn't remember! There were some fuzzy memories of soccer games and tee-ball in their backyard when they were young. Others about trying to teach him to ski one year, and nearly getting him killed when they jumped off the ski lift too fast. But overall, it was a blur, nothing that really stuck.

This time, she had a feeling it would be different.

9

LUCAS

L ucas eyed his sister in the backseat with her awesome lizard creature. They had found her, but now all three of them were stuck. It wasn't like he had exactly expected to be able to log out right away, though, so that was fine. As long as he was with her, the three of them as it was, they would all have a better chance.

Together, they would be able to figure this out. And if it meant meeting this Simon figure, so be it. As much as she liked to pretend to be the cool kid, he still remembered the way they used to make forts out of sheets and chairs, how they would hide in there with toy swords and pretend they were going to fight off an invading army. Then Dad would come in, pretending to be a cave troll, and they would laugh hysterically.

That was all before the man went missing. Back in the days when they still had a family. Now, riding with his sister, and seeing her with that same look of excitement she'd shown back then, he wondered if there was a chance he could have that sense of family again.

He had his sister back, after all. Not just physically, but all there.

"Now might be a good time to note that you have a sword, too," Fido said, though he didn't seem to know which of them to address.

"Fido?" Lucas asked.

"You named yours Fido?" Madison laughed. "They aren't dogs."

"That was all Jacob with the naming," Lucas pointed out.

"Although we could be," Fido said. "Dogs, I mean. The options are numerous, and we have some skill points, if you so desire."

"Really?" Jacob lit up. "I've always wanted a dog!"

"Wait, about the sword...?" Lucas turned to Fido. "We get swords like hers?"

"Just one," Fido replied. "It seems that you weren't both supposed to come through. Now that you're here, nothing can be done."

"One sword?" Lucas couldn't believe it. "What happens to the other person?"

"Maybe he gets the dog?" Madison offered, apparently trying to be funny. Jacob actually seemed to like that idea.

"And then maybe... I mean, Fido—are there spells in here?" Jacob asked. "If he gets to be the warrior, can I be the mage?"

Fido and Easter shared a look of amusement before the little furball said, "I think that could work."

"And these skill points?" Lucas asked, already turning back to his screen and noting that, yes, all of the fighting had brought him up to level two.

"You seem to be sharing the experience points, or XP," Fido explained. "While your sister is level four, you each are level two. So only one skill point each, for now."

A little scoff came from Easter, who had curled up on Madison's lap. She shrugged at Lucas's glance back.

He was fine with her going up levels faster than him —she was the big sister, after all. Her having more advantages was nothing new.

"Let's see," he said, turning back to his screen and looking over the various stats and ways to use skill points. It showed him having two strength and speed, and the same with other stats like defense, stamina, and the like. When he swiped to the skill points, he noted the areas to upgrade the furball and the sword. Skills and spells showed as well, but seemed locked out by higher levels or the need for more skill points.

"So I can use mine however I want to?"

"How are you doing that?" Jacob asked.

"Upper left," Lucas said, indicating the spot where it showed up for him, but noticed that he couldn't see his friend's screen. "I'm guessing you already did it, Madi?"

That's what he called her sometimes, to keep it simple.

"Yes," she replied. "Two points to my pal, Easter."

"Wait, you gave me a hard time for naming mine Fido?" Jacob asked, and laughed. "Easter?!"

Easter snapped at him but gave Lucas a wink.

"Okay, if I get the sword, I'm upgrading that," Lucas said.

"And I'm getting myself a dog," Jacob added.

"To be clear," Fido said, "I won't technically be yours, and—"

As he spoke, he suddenly transformed into a dog, as Jacob had apparently made the selection while driving.

"Please focus on the road," Madison said from the backseat.

"Well, this is rather pleasant," Fido said, and let out a bark. He sat in between the two front seats, but now stood and wagged his tail. "Ooh, quite fun!"

Lucas chuckled while selecting the sword upgrade. It gave him several options, including elemental damage, but he went with something called the "Volcanic Path." According to the description, while it started slow, as more points were added and it was upgraded, he could get full-on hot lava attacks from this sword. He liked the sound of that!

"Hey, um, isn't the trial supposed to be over?" Madison asked.

"I think so..." Easter replied.

"Then what's that?"

Lucas didn't see what she meant at first, but then the rumbling came, vibrating through his legs and next, his torso. He turned to see something rising up out of the ground. Massive, black wings that glowed purple, a torso that was part skeleton, part flesh. Then it spun its head toward them, and without a doubt, it wasn't just a dragon but...

...an undead dragon!

"That's not supposed to be here!" Easter shouted.

"Faster!" Fido added with a yip, then, "Lucas, blast it with everything you've got."

"Ahh!" Jacob shouted, continuing toward the building. They were so close now, but that undead dragon emerged and was charging over in their direction. The ground shook with each step.

Lucas worked the guns and every sort of weapon he could activate, pelting the dragon. A few shots caused it to stumble, but the thing was undead. How was he supposed to do anything against that?

Jacob swerved the car to avoid a blast of purple flames that came from the creature. The next time he swerved, they weren't so lucky though. The shot hit the back of the car, and the whole group went spinning. The car flew up and over, and Easter yelled, "Jump!"

They all went flying out and hit the ground rolling. Lucas looked up to see Jacob's health down to one heart, his own down to two. Madison had only lost half a heart, luckily. They were up and running again, with Easter moving faster, taking the lead. She led them to a series of rocks that stood tall against the mountain behind the nearby building. The dragon pursued, but soon they were able to lose it and had ducked down into a ravine to hide.

"We don't have to beat it," Jacob pointed out. "Just... make it to the building. Right?"

"It'll destroy the building!" Madison protested. "We'll be trapped, dead meat!"

"Actually," Easter interjected, "that building is where you will find Simon. I don't imagine the dragon will be able to touch him."

"Agreed," Fido said. "If anything, I would think the dragon is simply trying to stop you from reaching Simon."

"How's that possible?" Lucas asked.

"Rogue A.I., most likely."

Lucas nodded as if that made sense. "We make a run for it."

"What?" Madison shook her head, frowning and assessing the way. "That's gotta be like two hundred yards, versus a dragon. It has wings—can fly!"

"I'll distract it, you all go—" he started, but Easter cleared her throat.

"Maybe... maybe I can do a better job at that," Easter said. "After all, I am a helper of Simon's, assigned to get you to him. Maybe that will draw the dragon's attention."

"You can't," Madison said, hand to her chest. "We just started having fun."

Easter smiled, sorrowfully. "True, but... you three have to make it."

She looked at them, desperate, but Lucas had to admit this was their best bet. He simply smiled at her, even putting a hand on her shoulder. Oddly, she didn't brush it off as she would have before.

"We have an opening," Jacob said, and they looked to see that the dragon had its back to them.

"Go," Madison hissed to Easter. "But... try to make it back to me."

"I'll do my best," Easter replied, and shot off in the opposite direction while they all sprinted toward the building.

Lucas darted out ahead of the others, thrusting his hand forward. "How do you grab a sword? Like this?"

"Exactly, just wish for it," Fido said.

"What should I do?" Jacob asked.

"Run like hell!" Fido replied, running on all fours ahead of them. "Try to keep up."

Hand held out, Lucas focused on wanting the sword, and glanced over to see his sister with her sword already in hand. He stumbled slightly as his own sword suddenly appeared. It wasn't so heavy, surprisingly, but was about as long as his body was tall. Unlike hers, which glowed green and was generally silver, his was black with red glowing lines snaked along its blade.

He knew he didn't need it yet, but running with that blade in his hand made him feel more confident, made each step spring with energy.

"Feels good, doesn't it?" his sister asked. "Like we were meant to hold these things."

"Yes!"

"Hope you know how to use it," she added as she gestured ahead.

He looked to see what she meant, and saw five mini dragons rising out of the ground. These were pure skeleton, with red glowing eyes. They charged at Lucas and his crew, causing Fido to fall back, yelping. Madison charged ahead of Jacob and Lucas, and she was a sight to see. Every strike she made connected with the little jerks. So that by the time they caught up with her, two were already down and she moved for the third. Lucas stepped ahead of Jacob and Fido, not quite sure what to do but thrusting with his blade. He played enough VR to have the motion down, especially thanks to ones like the rhythm blade games. So when the small dragon darted out of the way, he was prepared and sliced back across to cut it in two. The little dragon's head lay on the ground, but the upper half of the torso turned on him and clawed over, so he ended it with a downward slice.

With the third one taken out by his sister, the final little dragon skeleton made a shrieking sound that caught the attention of the large dragon. Lucas glanced back to see that Easter was darting about the large dragon's feet with attacks, and seeming to be doing a good enough job of distracting it. Only, now it saw what was happening, and abandoned its attack on the little lizard.

"Get there now!" Lucas shouted as he and Madison charged the final little dragon together.

Jacob and the dog ran ahead, Jacob shouting about how he wished he had taken the sword.

"Hey now, that's not fair!" Fido said. "You haven't seen me at work yet. Level me up a bit more, and I can be a mount!"

Lucas got through one of the wings of the final little

dragon, but he was torn. He had thought that taking the little creature would mean getting a mount. Still, at least at this stage, having the sword was pretty awesome. Maybe later there would be a way to get Jacob a weapon, and himself a mount.

What was he talking about? There wasn't going to be much later. They needed to get out of this game, or simulation, or weird ultimate reality dream as quickly as possible. Too bad it was so much fun.

Madison joined him, so that both swords hit at once and sent the little dragon flying in a barrage of bones. They gave each other a look of respect and ran to catch up with their friend.

"I'm coming!" Easter said. Sure enough, she was moving fast to catch up. Surprisingly, even faster than the dragon.

As all of them closed on the building, they saw a figure approaching, a tall man in flowing robes with a long staff in his hand. At the end of the staff, a crystal glowed bright. It sent purple glowing light up into the sky, so that the light started to form a wall that moved down toward the approaching group. As they drew closer and closer, the wall moved down toward them. The dragon course-corrected, seeing that it wasn't going to be able to fly to intercept them. It landed with a thud and tore after them like a huge alligator. Each of its steps sent vibrations through Lucas, but they were almost past the purple wall. Jacob and Fido dove, clearing the wall, but Lucas turned and saw that Easter wasn't going to make it.

"Madi, your buddy!"

Madison turned and saw what he meant. "Don't stop for us!"

"Try and stop me." He turned as she did, sword raised, and flew back at the dragon. With a series of quick steps and jolting sidesteps, he was out of the way of one of the dragon's claws and hacking down with his sword. It clanged off of the beast's scales!

He spun, dodging a claw, and this time focused the blow, putting all his energy into it. The red glow intensified, and this time when he struck with his volcanic skill, a claw flew off and the dragon screeched.

Madison had the better shot, sword slicing right through one of the dragon's legs, so that it stumbled, sliding along the ground. She crouched down, picked up Easter, and ran. Together with Lucas, they slid under the last of the purple light that formed the wall between them and the dragon. The dragon hit the wall with a thud.

Madison, Lucas, and Jacob stood there with their little animal friends and turned to face the man that they knew was Simon.

10

MADISON

Madison stared at this man, and said, "Simon?"

Simon nodded, light fading from the crystal on his staff. "You have found me, and not only have you passed the trial... You dealt with this." He gestured at the dragon with the staff. "I must apologize, that was not supposed to happen."

"What is all this? What's going on?"

"Come, inside."

Madison and Jacob started to follow, but Lucas stood his ground.

"Lucas!" Madison said. "Come on, let's get this over with."

"Lucas?" Simon asked. "What seems to be the problem?"

"Are you serious? You basically stole us from our homes. Now you want us to follow you in there? I'm sorry, but we know better than this. You are a stranger... We need to go home."

"You're not wrong," Simon admitted. He cast an uneasy glance at the dragon. "We can do this here, if necessary. You have certainly proven yourselves."

"Do what exactly?" Madison asked, getting on the same page as Lucas.

"What I brought you here for, of course. Let me explain." Simon lifted his staff and again the crystal glowed, but this time it sent an image to cover the purple wall so that it became like a humongous movie screen. It showed a map of the world, and as they watched, it zoomed in on certain areas, and then flashed to others. There were deserts, forests, caves, and lakes. In some of the areas, monsters roamed. The monsters included zombies, goblins, mutated bears, and more.

"What are we seeing?" Jacob asked. "Don't get me wrong, it looks awesome."

"In many ways, it is," Simon said. "And yet... it needs work. See, I set up this world to be a sanctuary. The place of happiness. But an evil force has risen up against me and corrupted it. So I set up a recruitment tool of sorts, which is exactly what brought you here. You have proven yourselves to be warriors capable of ridding this land of evil. These monsters, and the ultimate monster controls... must be stopped. It is the same force that created that dragon."

"You brought us here to help rid your weird virtual-reality simulation of monsters?" Madison asked.

"Oh, child, it's so much more than that. This place is no simulation. It is real. It is another world, only accessible through certain portals, created with the help of electronic waves and those headsets you use. Many of the people that you will meet here, should you stay, are real. Many of the monsters as well. As you fight, you will be able to level up, to become stronger, and cultivate new powers you never thought possible. This will all be, in a sense, real."

"It sounds amazing." Jacob looked like he was about to explode with excitement. "Where do I sign up?"

"Right here." Simon pointed to a spot in the sky with his staff, and a button appeared there that said, "Accept."

Jacob took a step toward it, but Lucas intervened.

"We can't just abandon everybody back home," Lucas insisted. "Our mom needs us."

"I agree," Madison said. "As much as this is fun, and I'd love to stay... this isn't our lives."

"What if I could tell you that the time you spend here, will leave you rested? As if you slept? You come in here at night, when nobody knows, and you do battle.

You help. Maybe you save us all. There will be others, but why not let it be you? Nobody has to know, and during the day you can help your parents, go to school, or whatever it is you children do." Simon grinned, the twinkle in his eyes showing he knew he had them. "And here's the kicker... You know me, right? You know my wealth in your world. Whoever helps me rid this place of the ultimate evil, will have the ultimate reward. More money than you could ever dream of."

Madison thought of her mother, of all the problems they'd had since their father disappeared. And when she met Lucas's gaze, she knew he was thinking the same thing.

"Can we... go home and think about it?" she asked.

"I will allow this. But at night, hurry back. If you aren't here, I won't give you a second chance to return."

At that, and before Jacob could argue, the world faded around them and they were sent back to where they had come from.

Before Madison knew what was happening, she realized she was standing in the living room, holding the headset in her hands. She quickly set it back on the TV stand and sat down on the couch. She had to process all of this. Now that she was back in her living room, what she knew as reality, none of what had just happened seemed real. Could she have actually gone into the game? Had she actually raced a car, shot at enemies, and used a sword to hack at them and a dragon? It was too much. Like one of her brother's nerdy movies, or a dream.

It was late, too. She looked around, saw through the windows that it was almost sunset, and said, "Mom?"

"Madison?" Her mom came running in. "Is that really you?"

"Who else would it be?"

Her mom threw her arms around her, and said, "Where were you? Where is your brother?"

"He's not here?"

"I called the police and everything... They told me it hadn't been long enough, but I was so worried. I called your friends, but they said they hadn't heard from you. Same with Jacob, except his parents didn't know where he was, either. We started to think that maybe there was some big party or something. So...?"

Madison was about to answer, not sure what she would say, but then the door burst open and Lucas came running in.

"Mom!" He turned to Madison and grinned wide. "It was all real, wasn't it?"

"I guess it was." Madison turned back to her mother, who stood now and was glaring at Lucas.

"Don't you ever scare me like that again," their mother said. "You have no idea what it's like... No clue what it means to be up worrying."

"I'm sorry, Mom," he said and threw his arms around her. "I'm just so happy we're all back."

"Yes, well, I ordered Chinese..." That explained the delicious smell from the other room. She looked at them with concerned, wide eyes and asked, "Are you two hungry?"

Lucas and Madison shared a look of excitement, then both nodded enthusiastically. They all sat down for dinner and enjoyed their food, and when it was gone they got ready for bed. It wasn't until their mom was in the other room brushing her teeth, that Lucas and Madison had a chance to finally discuss what they'd been through. They snuck into the living room to not be heard.

"Thanks for going in," she said, tussling his hair. "My little bro, saving me?"

He laughed. "You saved me as much as I saved you."

"Sure."

"So... are we going back?"

They stared at the VR headset, both knowing the answer to that. Of course, they would go back in. How could they not?

With brother and sister standing side by side, they knew this was going to be epic.

11

LUCAS

For the first time in the history of Lucas, he had brushed his teeth, washed his face, and changed into his pajamas. When his mom came to ask him to get ready, he was already in bed with a book. It was upside down, he realized, but he quickly set it aside so that she didn't notice.

"Hey Mom, I'm beat."

"You... got ready on your own?" She put a hand to her chest.

"Yeaaah. Just, ready for the night," he replied. "I love you."

"And I love you, dear." She turned to check on Madison, then paused in the doorway. "You do know you're reading that book that used to give you nightmares, right?"

He glanced down and chuckled. The book he'd grabbed to look busy was called *Teddy Defenders*. It had been a gift from his godfather a couple of years back, but had been a bit creepy for him then. Considering that it was basically a superhero teddy bear that fights monsters, he wondered if maybe he would like it now, or whether maybe he was too old for it.

Anyway, he smiled, pretended to yawn, and rolled over in bed without a response. The door closed and muffled talking came from his sister's room. Meanwhile, he stared at the wall, eyes wide as he considered everything he had been through in that game world.

His mind was racing with memories of slaying the dragon. Well, working with Madison to do so, anyway. He couldn't believe how much his sister had kicked butt! She had never struck him as the kind who would get involved, much less be able to survive when the going got tough.

And then there was the invitation from Simon himself. More money than his mom would probably even know what to do with. Thinking of the smile on her face when she would learn she had nothing more to worry about made him giddy. Warm tingles ran up his legs and he even chuckled to himself.

Of course, first they had to win. He would do everything he could to see it through. With Madison and Jacob at his side, along with Fido and Easter, their chances weren't horrible. On top of all that, Jacob finally had himself a dog... kinda.

He lay there thinking about all this, waiting anxiously for his mom to go to sleep. Soon he started thinking about school the next day, and how he could possibly sit through a normal class after participating in a real-life battle race. Even Claude the cool kid would seem so boring after the game adventures.

"Psst," Lucas heard, then blinked, realizing his eyes had closed.

"Wha...?" he muttered, turning in bed and seeing his sister in the doorway.

"Tell me you didn't fall asleep."

He sat up, rubbing his eyes and trying to clear his mind. "I don't think so... or don't remember sleeping."

"Come on. Mom went into her room, so now's our chance."

"Oh!" He shot up, then rearranged his blankets in case his mom came in to check on him. Better to not let her know he was missing.

"Good thinking," Madison said, and tip-toed back to her room to do the same.

They met in the hall, both sneaking past the door to their mom's room. Light shone out from the crack at the bottom, so she clearly was still awake. That was fine, though, because in less than a minute they would be gone. Was it sneaking out if they only left through a videogame? That was a toughie.

Madison reached out and took Lucas's hand as they entered the living room.

He pulled his hand away, frowning as he hissed. "What was that?"

"In case you're scared." She shrugged. "Like when we were little."

"I don't see what there's to be scared about."

She pursed her lips, then grinned. "Me too, this is too awesome. When I saw you driving up during that zombie battle—"

"And you with that sword?" He mimicked her slicing through zombies. "You were on fire! Not literally, which I feel is worth stating since there was a dragon."

"Right. The dragon." She nodded, wide-eyed. "This... Simon guy, you think he's for real?"

"I hope so."

"For real. Our whole lives could be changed. This is the golden ticket."

"The what?"

"You know, chocolate factory..." She waited, but he really didn't seem to be following. "Never mind. More story education I need to fill you in on when this is over."

"Deal."

"Hurry up then, turn it on. Did you check in with Jacob yet?"

"Oh, right." He hit the on button on the headset, then went for his cell—charging on the kitchen table, and texted: *Dude, you up?*

A text reply came almost immediately: *Already have everything on and ready. Took a piss break and all, in case.*

Heading in, Lucas texted back, then put the cell down.

Lucas had taken care of business right before getting in bed, so was good to go. He gave Madison a nod to say it was go time, and together they picked up the headset and grinned at each other. The green light flowed out and around them, and once again they were whisked away to this other world.

A cool breeze hit them with a spray of water, which came as a surprise. It jolted Lucas out of any remaining drowsiness, at least. The two were standing on a metal platform in the middle of the ocean. Nothing but water in all directions, at least at first glance. As they looked, though, there seemed to be an area in the distance where the water fell inward from all sides in a square shape.

Jacob appeared, finally. "Whoa, this is crazy."

Realizing his friend wore a tunic and britches with a cloak over it like in their videogames, Lucas looked down to see he was dressed similarly.

"Good to see you," Lucas said, giving him a fist bump. "But where...?"

He didn't need to finish the question, because Fido stepped out from behind him, and then Easter had stepped out from behind Madison.

"This is strange indeed," Easter said.

"Hey guys," Jacob said, kneeling to pet the dog's head. Madison had done the same with her large lizard.

As Lucas felt left out, he reached for his sword and was glad when his fingers gripped its hilt.

"This must be like the next level," Lucas said, eyeing their surroundings.

Madison frowned. "But I'm level four, and you're each level two, right?"

"Not that kind of level," he corrected her. "Like, when you're in the first part of a game, then beat it and move onto the second, and on and on."

"Ahhh." She nodded, catching on quick. "So before we had racing and zombies. What now? And... what is this place?"

"More importantly, what are we supposed to do. Swim?" Jacob turned to Fido. "Do you know the answer to that?"

"Sorry, no," the dog-like fluffball replied. "My job was to get you to Simon. The rest is up to you."

Easter grunted in agreement, but then pointed with one of its claws at the sky behind them. They all turned to see that large, green "Accept" button floating in the sky.

"I guess we're doing it, right?" Jacob said.

"We're here for a reason," Lucas replied, and he reached up to press it.

"All at once," Madison said, hand up next to his, and they waited for Jacob. After a moment's hesitation, Jacob thrust his hand up, then all three together touched it. Nothing happened, other than the button fading away.

They all shared looks of anticipation and confusion, then jumped in surprise as Simon appeared in front of them. His staff was glowing, a ball of what looked like water floating around his base protectively.

"I pulled a lot of strings to get you here," Simon said as he floated over to them. This time he wore a long, black coat complete with blasters tucked into belts and holsters. On his head was a wide-brimmed hat, similar to pirate fashion. "And I'm so glad you chose to accept."

"Great, thank you," Madison said. "Now, care to explain where we are?"

Simon nodded. "The rogue artificial intelligence, or A.I., has decided this is where it is keeping a key that we need, to access the inner gates that keep us from destroying it. You get that key, you get us moving toward our first step to victory."

"And why can't you get it?" Jacob asked, causing

Lucas to cringe.

"It's okay to ask," Simon replied, apparently reading Lucas's thoughts. "See, this A.I. and I have a special sort of connection. By this I mean, it's able to affect me differently than you all, but I'm able to attack it in ways you can't. For example, getting us here, and this." He waved his staff, creating several small ships. Each sailed a pirate flag with skull and swords crossed—except on second glance, they weren't swords or bones, but magic staffs like his own. "I can create these, with NPC crews, and help you get to the labyrinth. From there, it's up to you."

"You want us to sail these?" Jacob asked, eyes wide. "We've never sailed."

"With a crew, as I said. It'll be as easy as playing a videogame—you steer, you aim, and you fire."

"Fire at what?" Lucas asked, but as soon as the words left his lips, his answer came. It was in the form of a cannon shot exploding, then the blast of water that erupted from where the shot hit. Not close, yet, but they all turned to see a line of ships sailing their way from the square spot in the ocean.

"Where'd those come from?" Madison asked.

"The A.I. has found ways to fight back." Simon gestured. "Go forth, young warriors. Show me that I have chosen you three wisely."

Lucas squinted at that, but let it go. Technically, he

had only chosen two of them—Madison had sort of snuck her way in off of his victory, but that was fine. She had certainly proved her ability to survive here.

There were three ships, so this time each kid got their own. It was at times like this that Lucas wished he had a pet like the other two did. Still, as he boarded his ship, a hearty greeting rose up from his pirate crew. Even though he knew they were all NPCs, he had to admit to the beating in his chest because they made him nervous. These were full-grown men and women, pirates of the most vicious sorts. Some looked straight out of *Peter Pan*, with flashy colors, stripes, eyepatches, and peg legs. Others reminded him of the old *Treasure Island* book cover, or the *Pirates of the Caribbean* movies.

How strange, then, that they all awaited his command. At the moment, the only sailing words he could recall came from *The Princess Bride*, so he said, "Hoist the thing! And the other thing!"

"Aye-aye, Cap'n!" the largest of the pirates replied, and then turned to get the men working. Soon they were moving out, the crew singing in that chanting way that made him almost able to believe he was back in the old pirate days and he was actually captaining a ship.

He glanced over to see Madison's ship on one side, Jacob's on the other, the three of them sailing out against a force at least four times their size. Time for another grand adventure!

12

MADISON

Another shot rang out, causing Madison to look to Easter. "What do I do here?"

"You're doing fine," Easter replied, lizard tongue slipping out to taste the wind. "When the fighting starts, just make sure you're steering out of their lines of fire, and shooting at them whenever possible."

She gulped. One thing her dad had always known about her that they had managed to keep from the rest of the family was her fear of water. As long as she kept the ship from sinking, she would be fine. Still, being surrounded by all that water and its seemingly endless depths didn't fill her with comfort.

The next shot that came hit too close for comfort, so

she took the wheel and started to break right, giving her brother room to navigate. She thought of calling out orders, but really had no idea what she was doing. A large woman with a red bandana and hook in place of one hand was marching up and down the deck barking out orders anyway, and they seemed to be getting the job done.

One pirate ship had turned at an angle, and a warning shout came from Madison's crew. She started turning the wheel, then realized she was already at a good shooting angle, so opened fire. At the same time, bursts of red and orange showed from the other ship, black smoke rising. Balls and chains ripped into Madison's ship, and her shots hit the enemy.

"Reload!" a shout came from below, but Madison had no intention of keeping the ship in place. She went full sail and pushed on, firing only once again as she moved out of the enemy's line of fire. One of those last shots took out the enemy's mast, and her crew cheered as one.

More enemy ships were moving into position, though, and two were trying to blockade their advance. Without a doubt, she was going to have to fight.

"All right, ladies and gents," she shouted, "what's the best move here?"

"Cap'n?" the lead lady asked.

"I want to push through those two there to reach that square as quickly as possible, while arriving with my ally ships intact. What's the best way to do that?"

"Charge 'em!" one of the other pirates shouted.

The big lady shrugged. "Could work. Another plan would be to slingshot ourselves around."

"What?" Madison shook her head, laughing. "That would never work. The physics alone—"

"You're talking in your world, Cap'n," the lady interrupted. "Here... it'll work."

Madison arched an eyebrow, unsure.

She saw a pirate manage to board Lucas's ship and was just starting to worry, when she saw him swing his sword and send the man overboard to pixelate away before hitting the water. He was probably glad he had an upgraded sword in that moment, and since his screen had popped up, she assumed he had leveled up.

Speaking of leveling up, she thought, she still hadn't used her last skill point from reaching level four. As she turned the boat again, she pulled up her screen and gave it some thought. It would be a good minute before the next ship came into range, and she was learning that ship battles could be a lot slower than she had thought, based on movies.

That gave her time, and she decided to upgrade her sword, too. As she assigned the point, she figured that extending its reach was always a good thing. No matter how big that sword was, she knew she could handle it—the thing was like an extension of her soul. When it was upgraded, it showed an added bonus of a "Shock-wave Attack," which she figured meant it would send off energy waves to extend the reach of her strikes. *Nice!*

A glance showed that they were coming up at an angle to fire on the enemy, so she gave the order to fire, followed by, "Do it. Slingshot us."

The lady grinned and gave the orders, while Madison turned to her friendlies and called out, "Stay close, and mimic what I do!"

She wasn't sure they had heard her, but since the other two ships moved over toward her tail, she assumed they got the idea. All three formed a triangle, shooting to clear the path as they went. Just when it looked like they were going to ram the blockade, the pirates ejected massive grappling hooks from the side of the ship. The hooks connected with enemy ships that were trying to move in for the attack, catching hold of them. Both ships were suddenly strained, pulling against each other, but then another order was given and Madison's ship cut the hooks free. It sped out and around, barely skimming over the water in a way that Madison knew was quite impossible but enjoyed nonetheless. This movement sent the ship out to the side and around the blockade, giving Madison and team a clear path to the square.

A glance back showed that Jacobs's ship had made it, but Lucas's stopped short.

"We have to take out the blockade," she ordered, and then opened fire on them from the rear. "All hands, obliterate them! Make a path for my brother!"

The attack that followed was an onslaught of the two pirate ships led by Jacob and Madison, sinking the first ship before Lucas even got close. Then Lucas and the second were firing on each other while the rest of their fleet tried to catch up.

"Provide cover fire!" Madison told her crew, while Jacob went to help Lucas with the second blockade ship.

Madison lobbed shots at the approaching ships, so that if they approached too fast, they were hit. She had to imagine this was so much more fun than how real pirate battles had gone down. Finally, Lucas was through, the second blockade ship in flames. Madison turned her ship back to join the other two, and they dropped charges as they made for the square drop-off point.

"Get to the entrance!" Simon shouted, voice booming out over the ocean. "You have to get down there!"

Down there? She turned back to him in panic,

though he was too far away and wouldn't see the look in her eyes. How could he expect them to sail over the edge? He had to be crazy. It wasn't until they were growing close that she even truly started to process their plan.

But by then it was too late, and not like she was going to change the plan, anyway.

"It's been swell, pirate crew!" she said, not really knowing how to say goodbye to a bunch of NPCs who were about to cease existing. "Enjoy the ride!"

"To our captain!" a shout rose up, followed by cheers.

As the ships reached the edge, it was like sailing over the side of a massive waterfall. She wanted to scream, even knelt and wrapped her arms around Easter, holding her tight as they went over. But the strangest thing happened—the ships started to transform! For a second she thought they were breaking apart, but then they started to change, turning into what were basically large surfboards with sails at the back like parachutes to slow the fall. The pirates all floated up and pixelated away in a strange moment of Madison not being sure if she was supposed to be sad or not.

"What do we do here?!" Madison shouted.

"SURF!" Jacob called out from nearby, and

apparently, he knew how to do that, because he went zipping past her, with Fido by his side.

"You can do this," Easter said. "And if you don't..." Already the surfboard started to topple, and she nearly went flying. "Just do it!"

She took a gulp, reached down deep for her courage, and pushed herself up with Easter still clutched tight. Letting out a loud warrior's battle cry, she braced herself and set her legs shoulder-width apart. Somehow, she was surfing down a waterfall, going vertical, and headed right for an area below that was slowly coming into view. The maze was right there, she realized! Several walls became visible, with their windy paths and dead ends.

Aiming for it, she whispered, "Don't let me die."

"I'll do whatever I can," Easter replied. "But right now, you need to focus, we're going off track from your brother!"

"What?" she looked around and, sure enough, they were going toward one section of the maze, he for another! Jacob seemed close to her, but as the maze rose around her, she realized it was too late. All three of them were landing in different sections.

The sail flew out like a parachute as the surfboard went horizontal, then she was skidding along it through a stone corridor, tall cobblestone-looking walls on either side. The surfboard came to a stop, and she went rolling, slamming a shoulder against one of the walls. Half of one of her hearts went away. Considering that she had four now instead of the original three, that wasn't so bad. But she worried about the guys with their lower levels. Maybe not Jacob, as he seemed to be a natural on that board.

"Easter?" she asked, looking around for her lizard friend. The passages were dark and cold, a slick substance reflecting faint, green light.

She finally spotted Easter clinging to one of the walls. The lizard cocked its head, eyeing her, then said, "I don't like this place."

"You're scared now?"

"Hey, you get water, I get dark, creepy confined places that are controlled by evil A.I. beings."

"I have to give you that, I guess." She stepped over and held out her arms to catch the lizard, then let Easter crawl up onto her shoulder. The action pulled her hair, but she was surprised by how light the lizard was. And while it was like that, she noticed something else, too—she could suddenly see much better in the dark!

"We're sharing a connection," Easter explained. "When we're close, it should affect you. At the moment we're touching, so if you didn't notice any change, I'd be worried."

"I noticed," she said, sword out, glancing around to

decide which way to go. "We need to find my brother and his friend."

"Agreed."

"Any bright ideas?" She eyed the walls—too high to climb. "If I called out for them, it might draw monsters to us and—"

"Lucas! Madison!" Jacob's voice called from not so far off.

"So much for that precaution." Madison looked around, trying to gauge the direction his shout had come from. "

"Guys, I don't like this!" Jacob spoke up again, and this time Madison was paying attention.

"This way," she said, forgetting Easter was clinging to her back so didn't need to be told.

They charged around the first corner and found themselves face to face with a zombie spider. Basically, a zombie upper body with eight legs. As soon as it saw her, the zombie spider charged. Easter went into attack mode and Madison had her sword ready—except, there wasn't enough room to fully swing the sword in that passage! The walls were too close—though at least there wasn't a roof overhead.

As Easter moved around to the side and struck at its legs, Madison stepped back and attempted to bring her sword down on the spider zombie. Only, it dodged easily enough, and she almost hit Easter!

"Sorry!" she shouted, but then dropped her sword as the spider zombie lunged at her.

Fighting out in the open with full movement had been one thing, but this was terrifying. She saw Easter leap onto the creature's back and strike with her claws, but all it was doing was annoying the creature. This A.I., if that's what this was, really didn't want them here.

Madison pushed back, and the spider crawled away. She wasn't sure what to do here, so simply kicked and shouted, trying to either surprise it or scare it off. Neither worked, and then it was stepping on her with multiple feet, its face coming in close to bite her.

She had an idea. Instead of trying to push it off, she simply held her hands between herself and the monster, then summoned her blade. BAM! It was in her hands a split-second later, no swinging necessary, as the blade had appeared right in the middle of the spider zombie. The monster froze in place, then collapsed onto her and the blade. She dismissed the blade and shoved the monster off, glad that it pixelated away instead of being all gore and nastiness. Her XP shot up quite a lot, bringing her close to the next level, but not quite there.

Catching her breath, she knelt, hand out and stroking the back of Easter when she came over.

"That was... intense," Madison whispered.

Easter nodded. "Only the beginning, too. Are you ready for more?"

"We have a whole labyrinth ahead of us, don't we?" Madison stood with a sigh, helping Easter back onto her shoulder again, and summoning her blade. She was going to hold it out in front of her from now on, in case anything came charging her way.

They took a left, then went down a long corridor while hoping to hear more calls from Jacob or Lucas. So far, nothing.

After her fourth turn, the terror was starting to subside a bit. In some ways, this could be almost fun. It started to remind her of a cardboard maze she remembered at the local watermelon festival a couple of years back. Sure, the cardboard version hadn't had monsters or the stench of rotten oranges that she picked up on more than once, but it was that same idea. Another turn and she noticed bright lines of light, reminding her of a hay maze she had enjoyed on their trip to a farm the year before.

Except, one step into the light and the click that followed showed her this was entirely different.

"Duck!" Easter hissed, and sure enough, a group of what looked like vampire ducks flew out at her from an opening in the wall above. They had massive fangs growing out of their beaks, and talons on their webbed feet, worse than any sort of bird she had ever seen.

She didn't bother trying to strike, but simply ran. They pursued, but Easter slashed one out of the sky, and when Madison turned a corner and then another, a wall went sliding up behind her. Weird, but welcome.

That didn't stop her from running, but she slowed when she heard Jacob's call again. She went stumbling out around the corner and stepped on a stone that clicked. Her first thought was that it was going to be like in *Indiana Jones*, with darts or something shooting out. Instead, all it did was open a wall to her left. Fido saw her first and barked—even though he could talk. Beside him, Jacob was running away from two little jelly blobs, shouting, "Stay away, stay away!"

"Easter," Madison said, "the pressure plate!"

"On it," Easter said, and jumped off to stand on the plate. Luckily, the large lizard weighed enough to keep it down.

Madison darted over to Jacob, sword appearing to stab the first jelly and watch it vanish. Her XP bar rose by a bit, but they clearly weren't worth much. She indicated the opening and shouted, "Get back, through there!"

As they went, she stabbed the second, and looked up to see a whole group of more jellies moving toward her. They were on the floor, walls, and ceiling. She checked to see that the others were through, then went back after them and scooped Easter up again.

The wall closed as several jellies tried to make it through, squishing them in the process.

"Yuck," she said, then eyed Jacob. "You good?"

He nodded, then looked over himself, patting down his body to check. "Looks like it."

"Good. Come on, we have to find Lucas."

They moved on together to look for him.

13

LUCAS

Lucas had arrived in the maze to find he was alone, which sucked, but he was too excited to focus on that. He would find his friend and sister, he had no doubt about it. After that awesome pirate fight and then basically vertical surfing to get down here? He was having a blast!

And now he got to be in an actual real-life maze! Well, the 'real life' part was debatable, but it certainly seemed real. When he met the first monster down here, he couldn't even fight it at first, being so excited to see this strange frog-like creature holding an ax. It wasn't as cool as the dragon, for sure, but he had played so many games where he got to run around in a maze that this was a dream come true. The creature's slimy, green skin shimmered in the faint light, its beady little black eyes staring at him.

"So... what now?" Lucas asked. "Are you going to attack, or...?"

When the creature simply stood its ground, Lucas thought maybe it would be his friend. But when he took a step forward, the creature lifted its ax to attack.

"Ah, I get it. You're blocking this route—so maybe there's something cool back there? Like a treasure chest?" Lucas pulled his sword from thin air. "Perfect. Let's do this."

His sword wasn't as large as his sister's, thankfully. He couldn't imagine how she was fighting down here with a humongous sword that was almost the size of herself. As the frog-creature leaped and came down with an ax strike, Lucas stepped forward and swung back, thinking he would easily strike the creature as it landed. Instead, the frog rolled in the air and kicked off of a wall.

"Whoa!" Lucas exclaimed as he nearly took an ax to the head but managed to pull back enough to barely avoid it.

He laughed as he came in with a thrust, then pulled back to block. When the next strike came, he parried and then slashed up and through the frog, causing it to pixelate away. Nice, but even better, it dropped loot! As

Lucas's screen showed an XP increase, the ax clattered to the ground. Lucas picked it up, figuring he could fight with a sword in one hand, and an ax in the other.

Best of all, his screen showed him going up to level three! A quick screen popped up to show stats increasing, but there was no time to check it at the moment. It vanished as he moved on.

He turned a corner and found a hall full of little goblin-like creatures, some with scrunched-up faces, others with faces kind of like donkeys. All had red eyes that darted over to him, and all raised steel to fight him.

For about a second, he felt panic, but then he realized something. These were likely kobolds, and if he had learned anything from videogames, it was that these creatures weren't so tough. There was a reason they needed such a large number. But in a narrow passage like this, not more than two or three could get to him at once. So instead of worrying, he saw this as the perfect level-grinding opportunity. He was going to get himself some XP!

Sword in one hand, ax in the other, he let out a warrior's cry and charged into the fray. Swinging strikes left and right, he blocked, connected, and destroyed. His XP bar shot up as he progressed through that walkway, until soon he had hit level four! He took a step back to process that his strength and defense were now at seven points each, and he'd received his fourth heart for health points. The skill point would have to be applied later, because more kobolds were coming his way.

He nearly slipped and looked down to see loot from the now-pixelated-out kobolds, including the shield he had nearly tripped over. It was nice knowing he had the option of that over the ax, but he liked fighting this two-handed way. A thought hit him, though. His stamina wasn't so high that he could do this forever, and more of those kobolds kept coming. So instead of continuing the fight, he took out two more, then got a running start and leaped onto the shield. As he had hoped, it sent him flying down the hall, the round metal part of the shield working like a sled. It was bumpy over the uneven stone, and he had to duck to avoid a kobold's arrow, but then he was past the main group before the shield hit and turned up, throwing him.

A kobold turned in surprise to find him barreling into it, both of them falling to the floor. He struck with his sword, used it to push himself up, and then looked back to see that only a couple of the kobolds had even realized where he had gotten off to.

He grinned, then ran. Twice he stopped to cut down his pursuers, and the third time he paused to check, he found he was alone.

Not only that, but he noticed the screen lingering there, showing that last kill had brought him up to level five! Unless his sister was doing better than him, that would put him above her level. He charged on, excited to gloat about the good news.

14

MADISON

J acob and Madison reached their fourth dead end, and it was starting to annoy her. They needed to find Lucas, but Jacob kept slowing her down, complaining that he was exhausted.

"Sorry, I just don't have the stamina you do," he protested the third time she told him to hurry. "I'm still only level two!"

"I don't think it has anything to do with that," she countered. "You're lazy!"

Jacob made an offended face, then glanced over at the dog creature to see if he would help him. "Don't listen to her, Fido. I'm not."

"Not my fight," Fido said, but grimaced as much as a dog could. "That said, we should probably start thinking smarter about how to find him."

"What did you have in mind?" Jacob asked.

Fido shook his head. "Nothing, but this clearly isn't doing it."

"Real helpful," Madison said, but then her face lit up. "Wait a minute—Easter!" All of them turned to the lizard as she helped lower Easter from her shoulder, holding the large lizard to look into her eyes.

"Yes...?" Easter asked, clearly uncomfortable with doing anything in this maze.

"I know you have it in you. You were on a wall, before. You could climb up, have a look around, maybe even spot my brother."

"Me, go up there by myself?" Easter's eyes went big. "You can't be serious."

"Oh, but I am. Fido's right, we need to think smarter here, and I think this is about as smart as we're going to get."

"I fail to see how that's my problem." Easter turned away from her, glaring at Fido. "Thanks a lot, you."

Fido took a step away, muttering, "Sorry."

"Don't get mad at him," Madison scolded. "This is about winning, right?"

"She's right," Jacob chimed in. "We have to finish the quest, and we're going to need Lucas for that. If you're our best bet, we have to count on you, Easter."

The lizard looked indignant, but slowly lowered her head. "Fine, I'll give it a try."

"You will?" Madison hugged the lizard tight. "You're amazing!"

She lifted Easter to give her a boost, then watched as the lizard climbed up the wall. Slow and careful at first, but then moving fast. Easter disappeared over the top, leaving the others to wait below.

"I'm sure he's fine," Jacob said, shifting back and forth uneasily. "It's Lucas we're talking about. Out of everyone I know, he's the best at these sorts of games."

Madison frowned. "You do realize this isn't exactly a game, right?"

"Sure. Yeah. What'ya mean?"

"Before, when Simon was explaining how this world worked... he said this was another world that he had discovered. That the game works more as a portal."

"Um, what?" Jacob scratched his chin. "I was kind of distracted by the zombies and dragons and all that. Plus, what you're saying doesn't make sense. How did he make the pirate ships and transform them, and the whole thing with them and the monsters pixelating away?"

"I don't know," she admitted. "Fido?"

The dog wagged its tail, considering the question. "I think it has to do with the rules of this other world, and how we're accessing it. Imagine if you had a room in your house that you digitally teleported to—"

"Not possible, that we know of," Jacob interrupted.

"Sure, but pretend. Now, imagine if, while teleporting, you were there but brought through digitally, and you could bring in other digital elements that affected the room. In a sense, you're sort of hacking that reality—but if the reality has a personality, or a being defending it, maybe that reality can fight back in the same way you're invading it?"

"You're saying we're invading this place, and the A.I. is simply trying to protect itself?" Madison asked.

Fido's brow furrowed. "I was simply trying to explain how it is we can be in a reality different from our own and be able to make adjustments to it."

"But you're not denying the invader part?"

This time, Fido snarled, then took a step away. "I can't... I don't know."

Madison scrunched her nose in thought, wondering what was up with the dog. It was like he had said something he wasn't supposed to, and was kind of glitching out now that she pressed the issue. She decided to leave it alone, for now, but her curiosity was certainly piqued.

"All I'm saying is," Jacob cut back in, "this place is too cool to be real. It's a fancy game, one that this Simon character clearly wants us to think is real... but I don't buy it. Hey, not that it matters as long as we get that money, right?"

"Maybe," Madison replied, but her attention was

already at the end of the hall, where a light pitter-patter sounded like wet feet on the stone.

Sure enough, a figure appeared in the darkness at the end of the hall, first lumbering past, then slowly returning to stare at them. It looked like a large frog with claws and fangs, and an ax slung over its shoulder.

It let out a shrill call, and then two more joined it, one carrying a bunch of chains that connected to small, round creatures. They were similar to how Easter and Fido had first looked, except these ones weren't hairy— they were slimy like the frog creatures, their skin patterned black and white, kind of like cows. Looking at them and their large eyes, Madison thought she was going to be sick.

As one, they charged forward to attack. Madison summoned her sword, charging forward to meet them as she shouted for Jacob to stand back. "I'll take the frog things, you and Fido deal with whatever gets behind me."

"What do I fight with?" Jacob shouted.

"Your dog!"

She wasn't sure that made sense or would work, but she was too focused on keeping them alive at the moment to worry about it. Sliding under an ax swing, she came up with a thrust of her sword, catching one of the frog creatures and sending shock waves out that struck the next one back. Round enemies behind them seemed to get stunned momentarily, though maybe not hurt. A cool effect, nonetheless.

As she pulled down with her sword, it clanged against stone. She found it easier to simply release it so that it faded away, then call it back with another thrust. In this manner she darted between them, striking and releasing, while behind her Jacob shouted out for Fido where to attack. She glanced back to see Fido take out one of the ball creatures, and Jacob caught one with a kick that sent it splatting against the wall.

"Way to go!" she shouted in encouragement, only to find her lack of attention meant one of the ball things caught her in the stomach. It sent her stumbling back, all the wind knocked out of her. When another ax strike came her way, she almost didn't avoid it, to the extent that the flat side hit her against the shoulder and sent a shock of pain through her right side. Another reminder that this couldn't really be a game.

"Heads up!" Jacob replied, too late.

"Jerk," she muttered, then had her sword up to slice through the frog thing and send him pixelating away. Three of the silly round creatures jumped at once, one pummeling her side but two others meeting her sword as she held it back up for a block. This was more stressful than she had hoped it would be, but at least her XP was rocketing up.

"Axe!" Jacob called, and she spun, kicking the ax

that the frog that had dropped his way. As she turned to slice through more ball creatures, she saw Jacob in the fight, hacking at the other monster at her side.

She gave him a thumbs-up as she thrust at more of the creatures, then together they advanced on the two remaining frog things. As a pair, they were a force to be reckoned with, her going for the long-ranged strikes and then moving around attacks so that Jacob could get in short-range. He would hit them high, Fido hit them low. Their XP rose and they each leveled up, and then they had cleared the room!

She turned to high-five him when she heard the twang of an arrow and noticed the gleaming white of a skeleton just beyond him. A figure moved in a green flash—Easter had leaped down from the wall, knocking the arrow out of the air and landing with it.

With two quick strides and a thrust from her sword, Madison had the skeleton in a pile of bones that quickly pixelated away.

"Thanks," Madison said to Easter.

"Hey, don't thank me."

"Of course I have to. You saved my life."

Easter chuckled, which was weird coming from a lizard. "No, I mean don't thank me because the arrow was going for Jacob. He should be thanking me."

"Oh."

Jacob laughed nervously, then very seriously said, "Thank you."

"Any sign of Lucas?" Madison asked.

"There's good news, and bad news," Easter replied.

"Good news—yes. Bad news, he... well, there's no easy way to say this."

"No..." Madison put a hand to her mouth. "But he'll respawn, right?"

"Respawn...?" Easter's eyes went wide. "Oh, no, he's not dead. A spider caught him in his web, is all. He's struggling to break free as we speak, so... let's go!"

"Say that right away next time!" She motioned to the two directions of the hall. "Your punishment is you have to lead the way."

"Wouldn't she have to anyway, since she's the only one who knows the way?" Fido asked.

"Quiet, you."

Easter seemed braver now, though, having scaled the wall and saved them from a skeleton. When she took the lead, it was with her head held high, tall slithering along the ground, ready to sweep out the legs of her enemies.

Madison took each step anxiously, though, figuring they couldn't move fast enough. Her brother was caught in a spider's web! The thought made her sick, and the farther they went, the more her mind filled with images of cutting some jerk spider open.

15

LUCAS

Had Lucas seen Easter on one of the far walls, or was it another element of his imagination? Since the spider had started wrapping her web around him, he had begun to see things, and didn't know what was real anymore.

For instance, the massive bacon cheeseburger with barbecue sauce he could swear he smelled, and the thought that he could see on the floor below him. Was that real? Or the other bundles of web hanging nearby, could they really be there? Monsters who had fallen prey to this stupid spider like him?

He wanted to kick himself for being so foolish. For one, he had dropped the ax he had found for Jacob, and was pissed at himself. Second, he was quite possibly going to die here. He had thought he would be brave.

He saw a huge hornet-looking monster, charged it to get his XP up, and found himself snagged halfway there! The hornet had already been in the web, too, he just hadn't been able to see it.

And now what was he supposed to do? In theory, he could summon his sword, but his hands were in such a position—in front of him and under his chin—that he was worried he would stab himself if he did.

At least the spider wasn't anywhere in sight.

Lucas knew from watching insects caught in spider webs that the more they struggled, the worse it seemed to get. But he couldn't simply give in, right?

He looked around for an answer, then froze—two eyes stared at him from another bundle of web within reaching distance, if he'd had use of his arms. Large, brown eyes with dark eyelashes. A muffled sound came from that direction and the eyes shifted, as if trying to tell him something. He followed her line of sight and spotted another form to his left, barely out of sight. Whatever she was trying to communicate was beyond him, except that there was another person there. A glance back showed she was still trying to say something, but he shifted his eyes back and forth as if to shake his head. A slight shaking of his head actually came! He shook it again, and realized that, while his body was tightly held, his head could get somewhat loose. And then he saw that the other form to his left wasn't so well confined.

Now that he could turn his head, it gave him an idea. He shifted, moved his head out of the way, and hoped with all his might that he wouldn't cut his own chin. Summoning the sword, he shifted and was able to cut a line of web free. The other figure went swinging, part of the web breaking so that a hand reached out.

A second later, that hand had a jeweled dagger, cutting through web, and an Asian girl emerged. She gave him one look, eyed the way down, then jumped. Grabbing onto him, she said, "Thank you," then cut the webs around him half off before jumping to the next figure.

Lucas broke the rest of the way free, then saw the Asian girl jumping down to the floor with the other figure. He could now see the one with the brown eyes was a girl, too, with honey skin and frizzy hair. Both turned to him as he fell to their side and offered a sheepish smile.

"Got caught by the spider, too?" he asked, and immediately felt like a dufus. He couldn't have started off with something cooler to say?

"It's okay—happens to the best of us," the frizzy-haired girl said, then thrust out a hand. "Name's Ralli. You must be from Earth like us?"

"Guilty," he said with a grin, accepting her hand. He

turned to shake hands with the other girl, but she eyed his hand and turned away.

At his look of shock, Ralli chuckled. "Don't mind Christy, she sees this all as a competition. She only helps me out because our moms know each other and we figure we can split the prize."

"Oh?"

"That's not the only reason," Christy cut in. "Give me some credit. It's also because I worry you can't handle yourself."

"Ah, that. Pity." Ralli winked at Lucas. "We might want to move on before the spiders come back."

"Wait." Lucas glanced around. "Spiders as in... more than one?"

"I counted at least three."

He gulped, wondering if this was somehow karma for always being the one to deal with spiders back home. Then again, he was usually nice to them. If he could, he would always take them outside rather than squish them.

In this case, he was pretty sure squishing was in order—except that the one he had seen was about the size of a dog.

"Enough jabbering then," Christy said, and she led the way toward one of three tunnels.

It happened to be the way Lucas had come from, so he spoke up. "Not that way."

"Seriously?" Christy eyed her friend skeptically. "We're not bringing him with us."

"Hold up," Lucas said. "I happen to be very good at mazes, and helped you out up there. Maybe we stick together for a bit, right? At least until we're close to finding the key, then see what happens."

"See, he knows about the key," Christy pointed out. "I don't think we can trust this kid."

"I'm sorry, but why wouldn't I know about it?" Lucas found himself not liking this Christy girl so much. "Simon sent me down here, same as you, right?"

"Simon..." Christy seemed to consider it, then nodded.

"Ignore her." Ralli gestured to one of the other passages. "Well, we came from that way and know it's the wrong route, and if you say that one is wrong, too, then that only leaves one way to try."

Christy clearly didn't like having her route questioned, but went along with it, jaw clenched. She avoided looking in Lucas's direction, which made him even more uncomfortable. They passed through a stone archway and into a part of the maze that actually had a roof over it. Patterns covered the wall, in what looked like... flowers?

Not sure if he should find that interesting or creepy, he decided conversation would break the tension.

"What level are you two?"

"Level..." Christy nudged Ralli. "He really just asked what level we are."

"Something wrong with that?" Lucas was finding it hard to hide his annoyance now.

"It's a bit personal."

Even Ralli seemed to shift uncomfortably at this topic, so he went for a different tactic. "Since you're at the same point in the game-not-game, I assume it's not so different from mine. I was just thinking, nobody else has gotten the key, since Simon is sending us after it. But do you think others have tried and failed? I mean, we can't really be the first ones, right?"

"Could be lots have tried and failed," Ralli said with a shrug. "A maze like this, scary monsters and spiders... I wouldn't be surprised if others quit or simply couldn't survive."

"*Shadow Legends* hasn't been out so long," he pointed out. "I'd like to think I was one of the first to get so far—I put in way too many hours."

"Yeah, same here." Ralli smiled. At least her warmth was somewhat offsetting the other girl's chill. "So maybe we're the first? After that spider incident, I'm debating though... Maybe we should go back."

Christy nodded in agreement.

"No..." Lucas couldn't believe anyone would even consider giving up. "You made it this far. I mean, I want to earn that money, but... You can't be serious."

"Imagine if you'd been stuck like that in the spider web forever?" Christy said, for the first time looking more scared than mean. "Like, we don't know what would happen. Maybe you could never leave the game? And we feel pain here, right? So... what if it was basically months of being stuck like that, the spider feeding on you. Agh! I can't even think about it without getting chills."

"Whoa. I never thought about it like that." He walked in silence for a bit, trying to get that creepy thought out of his mind. "But... still. This is too awesome to leave behind."

Clicking sounded from the halls ahead, along with the distant sound of swords clashing, he thought. Now that he knew there were others down here, he didn't want to get his hopes up too quickly that it might be his sister and Jacob, but still, he picked up the pace.

"You two do what you have to, but I'm staying."

"Then so are we," Ralli replied, catching up and motioning for her friend to stay close. "Maybe you're right, maybe we should all work together."

"Yeah?"

She smiled, and he couldn't help but stare—her smile was cute, with little dimples in her cheeks.

"And thank you, for helping us out," Ralli added.

"Yeah, same to both of you."

Christy muttered, "Thanks."

It was as good as he was going to get from her, and he was fine with that. And considering that the clicking sound was growing louder as three bone-white forms appeared at the end of the passage, there wasn't time to dwell. He summoned his sword, eyed Christy with her daggers, and saw that Ralli had pulled out a magic staff not so different from Simon's.

"Mage?" he asked.

She grinned. "You caught me."

At that, he led the charge. Several arrows shot out at him and spells from Ralli repelled two, while he dodged the third. Christy ran up behind him, and the two took down skeleton archers while Ralli hit the third with a stun spell long enough for them to take it out. In the last attack, the skeleton would have hit Christy if not for Lucas throwing himself against the creature, pinching his own arm but then getting his sword into place to end it with his sword's lava effect. His XP rose, but he wasn't anywhere close to getting a new level yet.

When he stood, Christy was eyeing him with an eyebrow raised. "You could've gotten hurt... for me."

"Maybe."

She nodded, then gestured for him to lead the way. "After you."

He rubbed his arm where it had gotten pinched but wasn't about to let her see his pain. Going ahead, sword raised, he noted more clicking and sounds from the passage to his left. A four-legged creature appeared. It was coming right at him, so he braced himself, sword held at the ready—and then saw three more figures coming behind it, two of them humanoid.

"Don't attack!" a voice said, and then he saw it was Jacob!

The creature scurrying toward him was Easter, and there was Fido running up with Madison at the rear.

"Guys!" Lucas laughed, then held up a hand as Christy stepped up next to him with daggers ready. "Oh, no. It's okay, they're with me."

She hesitated, but then lowered her daggers and conveyed the message to Ralli. He was glad to see that Jacob had found his own ax along the way, so didn't feel so bad about losing the other one. After quickly making introductions, they all greeted each other, but didn't have time to ask many questions before Ralli tapped him on the shoulder.

"Yeah?" Lucas turned, and didn't need her answer. Charging down the tunnel at them was a massive spider. Then, appearing on the walls and ceiling past it, at least three more! They all braced themselves, ignoring the whimper from Jacob, and prepared to fight the spiders.

16

MADISON

Madison had her massive sword ready in spite of her confusion. She wasn't sure how this fight was going to work now that there were five kids and the two animals. Questions about the new girls swirled in her mind, such as where the girls came from and why neither of them had an animal guide like Easter or Fido. Since the spiders were moving in fast, she figured she could wait. Answers would come in time.

"What's the plan, here?" the girl who had been introduced to her as Ralli asked. "You all normally attack in a specific way?"

"Honestly, we haven't had much of a chance to figure it out," Madison replied. "We were separated, so..." She looked deep in thought for a second, then said, "Spell caster hit 'em with all you've got, then move to the back. I'll stay with ranged attack in the middle. Yeah?"

"Good plan," Jacob answered. "Fido and Easter can watch our backs, and our feet—in case we're not looking down enough."

"No more discussing," Lucas said, "go!"

Without further debate, Ralli spun and shot out stun spells while the rest got into position. Madison stepped up and thrust out with her sword—they should have been out of reach, but her sword was so long and now had the extended strike ability. Shock waves went out and hit the closest spider, causing it to drop from the ceiling and fall, twitching on the ground. Two of the other spiders were within range, but she could only hit one, so went for the one in front of Christy. Lucas had a sword at least, which had a longer reach than Christy's daggers.

It worked; his sword hit the spider, chopping off half the legs. Only, it fell and lunged for Christy's feet. She was paying attention to another spider that had appeared, so Madison kicked the thing and sent it back down the tunnel. One of the other spiders leaped down, consuming it and then growing to twice its size!

"Wow," Christy said, seeing this.

"Gross," was Madison's reply. There had been a reason Lucas always dealt with spiders back home and not her. She was completely disgusted by the thought of being near them. Here she could almost imagine they were another monster in the mix, but this was too much.

When the massive spider came their way, she froze.

"Marrison!" Ralli shouted.

Madison was there enough to realize the girl got her name wrong, but not there enough to make her arms move. She was frozen in panic, heard her brother correct the girl on her name, and then felt someone pulling her back, pressing her against the wall.

"Stay with us!" Jacob said, holding her with one hand, ax in the other as his head swiveled around, checking for trouble. "We need you!"

She watched Ralli's stun spells going to work but it wasn't enough. Not just because the spiders kept coming, either, but because a groan sounded from the opposite direction. Then more groans. Her eyes slowly moved to see what it was and noted several zombies stumbling into the tunnel. They had spiders on one side of them, zombies on the other!

"I'm back," Madison muttered.

"Yeah?" Jacob didn't seem sure he was ready to believe it, still holding her. Oddly, he leaned in as if to kiss her.

"Totally read that wrong," she said, pulling away

and laughing. She'd always known the guy had a crush on her, but talk about bad timing!

"Sorry, but in games, that's always when it happens, right? Good cut scene, romance, kiss..."

"No. And this isn't a game." She turned to the zombies. "You all take care of the spiders, I'll do some damage against these hungry jerks."

"I got your back," Jacob said, ax up in two hands now. Fido went with them, while Easter stayed to help against the spiders.

Fighting zombies felt like the norm after the previous experience. She moved right in, only slightly disgusted by the rotting flesh smell or the pus. They were gross in their own way, but nothing like spiders. Plus, the moment she cut them down they pixelated out of there, so no big deal.

As an added bonus, they weren't as fast. Given her ranged attack and its bonus shooting, she was able to keep them at a safe distance. When one got remotely close, Jacob or Fido would do their damage. Their XP shot up, and she saw Jacob level up at least once. Her own XP bar was almost full, too, and she was grinning as it was about to level her up, too.

Her strike hit true, and she prepared for another, when something landed on her back! She shrieked, spinning and swatting at the furry body of a medium-sized spider. She got it off and then stomped on it, only to find her foot bounce back! She lost her balance and fell, looking up to see zombies incoming, overpowering Jacob while Fido darted between their legs yapping. She would remind Jacob to upgrade that dog, if they made it through this.

Lucas pushed back with the two new girls, forming a small wall of protection to push the zombies and incoming spiders back. As he fought, Lucas hit level five, and seeing that alone gave Madison hope. She pushed past her fear of spiders and rose, thrusting out with her blade along the wall to clear a path.

Catching on, the others started working in that direction as well, all moving slowly, but steadily. Each strike simply worked to keep their little bubble of protection, not much more.

"There're too many of them," she said, "we need another way."

"What other way?" Lucas shouted while kicking away spiders and hacking when he had room.

She didn't have an answer, but Easter did—the lizard was up a wall, swatting away a spider, and said, "I scouted—next room over is some sort of puzzle room. If we can get in there, that might give us a moment to rest."

"Get us to that room," Madison said.

"Agreed," Lucas replied, and the rest didn't argue.

"Follow me!" Easter said, moving along the wall in the direction they needed to go.

The others let out battle cries and charged, fighting with direction now. They pushed through and Madison reached level seven! She didn't have time to look at the stats yet, but if that next room really gave them a moment to relax, she looked forward to some upgrades. Now that she had felt panic, she thought maybe some defensive skills might make sense.

Turning the corner, they came to a large door with a fancy clockwork mechanism on it. Zombies and spiders were mixed in behind them now, but the group turned to fight.

"What's this door?" Jacob shouted, ax connecting with a zombie.

"Some sort of riddle, I'm guessing," Lucas replied. "And that means..." He turned to Madison, then went back to slashing at enemies.

She got the message. In school, she never shied away from math and subjects like it. She turned to assess the door, noting that the cogs were different sizes, but wouldn't move as they were—they didn't touch.

"I don't know..." she said, overwhelmed by it all. "It's like, they're not where they're supposed to be. Each one has different numbers, and there's a pattern."

"Figure it out!" Ralli said, casting her stun spells when possible. "I'm running out of juice here."

"Okay, okay..." Madison found that there were levers next to each bit of cogwork, and that if she moved them, it was like shifting pieces in one of those puzzles that required moving pieces in the right place to form the image. Only, there was no image here.

"Maybe the numbers mean something?" Lucas shouted.

The sound of fighting continued behind Madison, but she tried to focus. Considering that the cogs had different numbers of spokes, she imagined he was right. But how did it work? When properly arranged, there were only four cogs that seemed to matter, but the door had other numbers sketched into it, she now realized. She had taken them as simple design patterns, but no, they were roman numerals.

"Sudoku!" she blurted out, and was in her zone, analyzing the numbers and where they were in relation to each other. When she moved the cogs, some of the numbers around them moved, too.

And considering that some numbers stayed in place, she quickly started putting it together. Then she had it—each square of nine had to have one of each number, and when she finally figured out where the eight and the six went, it clicked into place.

The cogs started whirring to life, and the door swung open.

"Inside!" she shouted, and she moved aside,

summoning her sword to hold back the enemy while her group escaped within.

She was the last, slamming the door shut with a sigh of relief. Only one thing caught her eye as she turned with a smile, and that was the fact that Christy seemed to glitch for a moment. Running into the room, Madison thought she had shapeshifted into a bear momentarily, but then it was gone, and she thought she must have imagined it.

"We did it!" Madison said, grinning. The rest returned her smiles and commenced with fist bumps and high fives.

It was an empty room. Two passages led out of there, one straight ahead and one to the right. Madison went to check on one, Easter the other, but both were clear for the moment. Feeling at ease, Madison sat down to go over her stats and upgrades. Her defense and strength were each at fourteen now, speed at ten, and she had three skill points to use.

Analyzing her screen, she looked over what class options were available and saw one she thought looked especially cool—it was labeled "Shadow Hunter." As much as she never would have admitted to Lucas that she thought ninjas were cool, she had certainly imagined herself as one many times when back home practicing with her secret practice sword. The Shadow Hunter class had that appeal, with grayed-out skills further down the skill tree that could make her quite amazing.

For now, she chose an explosive shot skill that upgraded her sword's ranged attack. She also upgraded her defense. Next, she selected something called "Shadow Move," that she looked forward to trying out in combat.

Even though she had applied her skill points, she kept the screen open, looking over the various branches and skill paths available to her. If she was going to do this, she had to make sure she did it right. Everything was looking up. They had escaped into what they hoped was one more step closer to the key, and she actually believed they had a chance at beating this A.I. and claiming the reward money.

17

LUCAS

Lucas couldn't help but smile wide at the room, loving that it was empty other than his group. He was relieved to see no monsters in the room. As much as he enjoyed fighting, his arms were aching. Even after leveling up, his stamina wasn't infinite.

"Good! A chance to apply those skill points." Jacob said with a wide grin.

Since Madison was already upgrading herself, judging by her sly smile and the screen floating in front of her, Lucas decided Jacob was right. He pulled up his screen and saw that strength was at twelve, and decided to upgrade that to fourteen and used his last two points to go with a "Beastmaster" class track. For one, he didn't have a cool animal friend like the other two, so figured this might help balance that out. The first option was a wolf summon. He had always loved wolves, and always spent extra time watching them at the zoo. If he could have some wolves join him in battle, he would be on top of the world.

"How close do you think we are now?" Jacob asked, checking out his upgraded ax. "To finding the key, I mean."

"Easter, think you can have a look and guess?" Madison asked.

The lizard started scaling the wall, muttering something about always being the one who had to do it. As the rest took a breather, Lucas noticed Ralli and Christy whispering, glancing over their way more than once.

"We can't let them," Ralli said, probably louder than she had meant to be. Glancing up to see the others staring at her, she smiled and then walked over to Lucas. "This Simon guy, you trust him?"

Lucas frowned, not sure where this was going. Maybe Christy wanted to abandon them now to get the key for the two of them, but that didn't make sense with what Ralli had said.

"Lucas?"

"Ah, Simon? We don't really know him, but... he's a public figure, right? Can't just go back on his word, can he?"

Ralli pursed her lips in thought, then made eye contact with Christy for a moment before continuing. "See, what I don't get is why you would help him. You seem like nice people."

"But you're doing the same thing we are," Lucas countered.

"Are we?"

Lucas noticed his sister eyeing them suspiciously, hands in fists. She didn't trust these girls, after all they had been through?

"I mean, even if this place might be a reality in some strange way," Lucas replied, "it's really still just a game to us, right? Come on, some A.I. with the ability to interfere in this world is trying to unleash monsters and whatever. We stop it, this place becomes a better place."

"Except that it doesn't, Lucas." Her voice was slowly rising. "Not only does it become a worse place, but that jerk might destroy everything about it. He wants to merge it with his own somehow, to take ownership for power, and basically destroy our world!"

That last bit had been almost shouting, but the weird part of it had been one-word choice. "*Our* world?" he repeated back to her.

Everyone had turned to look then, and even Easter, halfway up, was staring back down at them. Ralli took a step back, magic staff held at the ready in front of her.

"Yes, that's what I said. This is my world, and it's me

—this A.I."

"What?" He was too confused to follow.

"I'm the A.I. you're after—and it's my key you're trying to steal!" She was almost shaking with rage. "I wanted to get to know you, see what sort of people are coming into my home, trying to do this to me, thinking I could lure you into a trap... and I have. But here's the thing, Lucas... I like you. So I'll give you a chance."

She held her staff up and a button appeared. It said, "Abort Mission."

"All you have to do is press that and you go home." She aimed the staff at each of them. "Or you can stay... and die."

"You... you're the A.I.?" He shook his head. "No, you're Ralli. I like you. I mean... this doesn't make any sense."

"It does, trust me." She took a step back and turned to her friend, who right before their eyes morphed into a massive brown bear. In one quick motion, Ralli was up on her friend's back, riding the bear with magic wand at the ready. Christy's daggers had become claws, and the bear had more just like those.

Lucas shared a shocked look with Madison, then Jacob, before turning back to the "Abort Mission" button and Ralli. He shook his head slowly, saying, "I'd like to talk about this, to figure it out... but we're not going home."

18

MADISON

Madison couldn't believe what she was hearing. The girl had annoyed her, and there had been that strange glitching thing with Christy looking like a bear. But to think that she had been the A.I. all along blew her mind.

"Wait," Lucas said, as the bear reared back, and Ralli held out her magic staff. "We're friends, I thought. We fought side by side! We can get through this, together."

"You're either abandoning the mission, or you're my enemy!" Ralli replied. "All that was a test—me trying to see who you really are. I created those monsters, much as your Simon has given you upgrades, race cars, and these familiars." She gestured to Fido and Easter with that last word.

Madison was fine with being enemies. Whatever. This girl wasn't about to give. Considering the path, and as much as Lucas maybe wouldn't like it, she only saw one option here—to attack before the girl took the initiative.

Sword thrusting as she summoned it, Madison went for her new skill right away in an attempt to catch the A.I. off guard. The bear pulled back so that the strike didn't land, though the extended shock blast hit Ralli and caused her to freeze for a second.

"Madi, no!" Lucas lunged, pulling her back as she went for the next strike. It would've landed if not for him.

"What're you doing?" Madison demanded, shrugging him off and preparing for another blow. "You heard her—this is it. She's given us an ultimatum, and if we want Simon to give us the money, we have to defeat her."

Ralli wasn't stunned anymore, and the bear was pacing, eyeing them and Jacob, who was frozen in place, eyes darting between the bear and the siblings. Madison got it—this was a tough situation, but she wasn't about to go back empty-handed.

"Way I see it, this A.I. is trying to trick us," Madison said, sword trailing the bear. "She knows what we're here for, and she's not simply going to let us take it."

"I don't care about the key," Ralli spat back. "It's only

one piece of the puzzle, anyway. You think I'd make it so easy? No! What I care about is that you, three kids who seem to be nice people, are trying to turn my world into some disgusting mutation. We have magic here, we have the ability to make something great—but Simon has his own ideas of what 'great' means, and he doesn't belong. You have to see this."

Madison prepared to strike but clenched her jaw as doubt worked its way through her body and down to her limbs. Enough so, even, that her sword started to lower.

"You see this, don't you?" Ralli said. "There's no need to fight. You can just go home, find some way to stop Simon from your end, and none of this ever happened."

"Except that it did," Jacob spoke up. "And someone's going to get that money... it might as well be us."

"Jacob?" Lucas stared at his friend.

"You know I'm right! Simon didn't only send us on this mission. He's recruiting kids left and right. And not kids, either, I'd bet. Anyone who can kick that game's butt, right? Soon there will be so many others down here trying to do what we're doing right now, Ralli won't stand a chance. Isn't it better that we get this money than some other jerk? Or worse, what if some gaming company or a government organization hires a bunch of pros to try and make it happen, once they get word of it? Like in that *Ready Player One* movie. We can't let that happen."

Lucas looked like he was going to be sick, but he nodded. "You might be right."

As far as Madison was concerned, he was. This A.I. was convincing, but this was a digital world, after all. If they were duped by her story and had to stay poor the rest of their lives because of their gullibility, she could never forgive herself.

"It seems you've all made up your mind," Ralli said, the bear growling. "Which means... we are enemies."

Without another moment's hesitation, she charged. But worse than that, the walls around them vanished, meaning they were surrounded by zombies and spiders. The trio and their animal friends braced themselves, all making quick eye contact to determine the strategy.

They knew how this worked by now. First with Madison's long-ranged attack, striking against Ralli at the same time as Ralli thrust out her staff. Both connected, but Ralli had gone for Lucas! He was frozen in place by a stun attack, same as Ralli! Which meant Madison could strike again, going for the bear. Having seen the first attack, the bear was ready and moved in, fast, knocking the blade aside.

Meanwhile, Easter and Fido charged out at the incoming crowd of monsters. As there were no walls, the spiders had to stick to the floor and were at a bit of a disadvantage. Zombies met Jacob and Lucas in battle, while Madison threw herself sideways to avoid the bear. It wasn't every day she had to dodge bear attacks, though it wasn't like the bear was larger than the dragon she had faced before. After that, she felt she could do anything.

"Make it quick!" Jacob said, and he lit up red while spinning, sending a power-filled strike in a wide arc at the zombies. Three stumbles back and then pixelated out, while several more clearly suffered damage.

"Nice upgrade!" Lucas said from the other side. "Watch this!"

With a grin, he made a fist that made a blue light glow, then what looked like two, glowing blue and translucent wolves appeared at his side. He laughed and pointed at the spiders, so that the wolf spirits attacked.

"Not bad," Jacob replied.

Madison agreed, but was too busy summoning her blade and trying to attack Ralli and the bear. Another stun hit Lucas, so that Madison had to focus her energy on defending him. Her brother's wolves moved back to help, but they faded away after a few seconds. Apparently, that summon spell didn't last long at his low level.

Seeing them, though, reminded Madison of her own recent upgrades. It was time to see what she was capable of. Her next strike pulled up something in her screen called "mana," and depleted a third of it as she thrust out with her sword at a group of zombies that was getting too close.

It was worth it! The blast from her sword didn't simply shoot out energy like before, but went into their midst and exploded! Five of them pixelated out and her XP jumped up. Then she was back on Ralli, swinging the blade around and trying her Shadow Move—another third of her mana drained, but black smoke rose around her. She darted left, and sure enough, Ralli couldn't seem to see her! The girl's eyes went wide, darting about in confusion.

The bear, however, sniffed with its nose. Madison knew she didn't have long before it sniffed her out, so she lunged—the blade connected and sent Ralli flying right into her zombies. As the girl's focus left, a glowing, floating box appeared not far off. It had to be the key!

"Ahh!" Ralli shouted.

The next strike hit the bear, and the explosion that took the rest of Madison's mana did the trick. As Ralli struggled to break free from her zombies, the bear was vanishing, and the girl started to pixelate out. A moment later, all that was left was the key. It floated there for Madison to grab. She reached out, took hold, and grinned as a surge like warm air filled her. They had done it.

19

LUCAS

Lucas still couldn't believe this was happening. His sister held the key! All they had to do now was tell Simon and find their way out of this place. With the key, he didn't imagine it would be so difficult.

A face appeared, floating as if projected by hologram. As it came into view, he saw that it was Ralli. She looked like she was about to cry. "Stop, please... This is my world. You can't destroy it. I beg you."

"I'm not trying to destroy anything," Lucas replied, turning to see her coming slowly down the hall, Christy back in girl form at her side. "But neither of you have exactly given us a reason to trust you."

"Please..." Ralli's voice was desperate.

Madison held the key but looked at it, confusion taking over her expression. "What if...?"

"What if she's telling the truth?" he asked. "Come on. You're saying Simon could possibly be trying to destroy this world, to use it for his evil master plan?"

"It's not so unlike him, actually," Jacob pointed out.

"What?"

"Well, in the past... he's kind of been known as the type of quick actor. Mergers and acquisitions, putting people out of jobs in the name of profits, stuff like that. He's not exactly Mr. Noble back home. Don't you read the news?"

"I'm certainly thinking about starting after this." Lucas ran a hand through his hair, trying to process this. He turned back to Ralli. "And you... do you have any way of showing us that what you're saying is true?"

"No...?" She held her wand and an image of mixed colors appeared there. "But I can show you the beauty of my world, maybe help you understand why it can't be destroyed."

The image morphed to show humanoid people living here in peace. This included a village filled with the bustling activity of shoppers at a market, a couple holding hands and staring out at the sparkling water of a nearby lake, and more. Another image showed animals leaping through fields—strange animals of vibrant colors unlike anything on Earth. Then there was the dive below the surface, where small, round creatures that looked just like Easter and Fido had done when they first met them, were moving around shimmering crystals and underground waterfalls. Something glowed down there, deep within, and Lucas felt he was being shown something with the utmost hope and trust. This was special, and in that moment, something touched him.

He was startled at first, but then looked down to see it was Ralli's hand. She held his, eyes staring into his eyes, pleading. As much as he felt for her, he still didn't know what the right move here was. Madison looked equally troubled.

"Jacob?" Lucas asked.

He shook his head. "I don't know."

"What if I could buy you time?" Ralli asked. "Go back, sleep on it, and you'll have a guaranteed fast-track back to me. Yeah? Maybe... maybe see how Simon treats you if you say you've changed your mind."

"And how do we know you'll bring us back in?" Lucas asked.

"What?"

"If we side with you, how do we know you won't close this place off forever?"

Ralli considered this, then her body started to form, and finally, she stepped forward, fully there again, and gave him a hug. When she pulled back, she was blushing!

"Consider that my promise. I like you, Lucas. I think we could all be great friends."

He really didn't know how to take that, but... nodded.

"We need time to think, to discuss it," Madison said, then nodded at the A.I. girl. "Okay, let's do it."

"Agreed," Lucas said, wanting to commit right then and there, but knowing they needed to talk about it between themselves. "Can you help us log out? Remember, if you try and trick us, we'll know you're what Simon says you are."

"Understood."

Ralli summoned her magic staff, waved it, and made a button appear in the air that said, "Logout."

"When you're ready to come back in, you'll do so the same way as Simon brought you, but... call for me. I'll be there, waiting."

All three kids took a moment, then stepped forward and pressed the button. In an instant, they were logged out.

20

MADISON

Madison stumbled as she found herself back in her living room, then turned to see Lucas with his hands on his head, eyes full of confusion.

"What do we do?" he asked.

A glance at the curtain showed light from what was presumably the sun coming up. What Simon had said was true, though, Madison felt as rested as if she had been asleep the whole night. If not for Lucas staring at her like that, she might have been able to convince herself it had all been a dream.

"Do...?" She chuckled, then laughed.

"Shhh," he indicated the hallway, where their mom was likely still sleeping. Since their dad had vanished, she never was much of an early riser.

"Only thing we can do," Madison said. "Go to school, give this some thought, and... then... figure it out."

"I can't go the whole day not knowing," he countered. "Are we siding with Ralli, or Simon?"

"He'll certainly expect an update tonight," Madison said. "Including, wanting to know why we didn't bring him the key right away."

"Exactly."

She rubbed her hands together, considering their predicament. If that was in some way actually a real world, which both Simon and the A.I., or Ralli, seemed to agree upon, how could they help give control of it over to Simon? Part of her didn't believe in other worlds or dimensions, but that was the same part that said physically going into a game was impossible.

In her mind, it was settled then. "We side with Ralli."

"Yes!" Lucas shot a fist into the air in triumph, then covered his mouth as their mom called out for them.

"What're you doing up so early... go back to sleep."

"Uh, just using the bathroom," Lucas said with a shrug, and Madison couldn't help but grin.

"Nice save there," she said, shaking her head while being sure to whisper. "I didn't know you felt so strongly."

"Neither did I, until you said it. As soon as the words

left your mouth, it was like I knew there wasn't another option. We have to help Ralli, defend that place from Simon and his other champions."

"Meaning we're rogue now."

He nodded. "Do we really have to go to school and all that? I mean, can't we just log in right now and be done with it?"

"It's almost morning. Plus, is Jacob on the same page?"

"I imagine so, but yeah, good idea to check."

She nodded. "And do it in person. Tonight, it's on."

He grinned, gave her a thumbs-up, and headed into the kitchen. "Want frosted flakes or granola?"

"Granola," she replied, following him in and watching as he poured two bowls, then got her milk and a spoon. When he handed them over, she arched an eyebrow. "Who are you, and what've you done with my brother?"

"Oh, that jerk who was always too preoccupied to spend time with his awesome older sis?" Lucas winked. "That guy is long gone. Just me and you now."

She chuckled, sitting across from him and starting to dig in. "Well, if you see him, tell him I said I like this guy way more."

"Will do."

The last thing she had expected when picking up the headset the day before was that she would go into a videogame world, decide to help an A.I. presence in their fight against one of the richest people in the real world, and form a bond with her brother that was long overdue. But here she was, and she loved it all. Well, maybe not the taking on the super-rich dude part. That terrified her. But she was ready and committed.

Every bone in her body was excited, knowing that the next night was going to be epic.

ABOUT THE AUTHOR

Justin M. Stone is a novelist (*Allie Strom and the Ring of Solomon; Falls of Redemption*), videogame writer (*Game of Thrones; Walking Dead; Michonne*), podcaster, and screenwriter. He has written on taking writing from hobby to career in his book *Creative Writing Career* and its sequel, and how veterans can pursue their passions in *Military Veterans in Creative Careers*. Justin studied writing at Johns Hopkins University.

To receive other free stories and audiobooks, as well as future updates, sign up for Justin's newsletter.
bit.ly/JustinMStone
And join my Facebook Group!
www.facebook.com/groups/JustinMStone

SAMPLE: GAME SPACED

Patrick stared at the massive spaceship, unable to believe he was going to fly into space. Unable to believe he had been selected to be one of the colonists of the planet which Earthers had labeled Gimline-8.

He preferred to think of it as Planet Gimli, because that sounded awesome. Gimli was a dwarf from the *Lord of the Rings*, one of the books he'd been able to find for free and therefore read about a quadrillion times. Any planet that had a name similar to a dwarf from his favorite fantasy series was fine by him.

"Don't worry, there will be other kids there," Sergeant Blimes said, standing at his side. "You'll meet plenty, and... maybe you'll learn to make a friend or two?"

Patrick smiled. Sure he would. It was one reason he had been selected to go—he didn't have much of a life on Earth to leave behind. He had essentially won the lottery, along with eleven other children all ranging from eight to thirteen. He was on the high side of that, at just twelve-and-a-half years old. They would join a couple hundred other would-be colonists for a multi-year journey through space.

Although, to say he had "Won the lottery" wasn't really true. They had all put their video game skills to the test, in the ultimate simulation of survival--a game of fully immersive VR that was unlike anything he had ever played before. The first step was to solve a series of puzzles, second was to stay in the game long enough to prove you could handle flight and zero gravity, and third had been to establish yourself in an in-game community.

He had done so, creating an Orc with a solid background, going on adventures and having a blast until they came to him with a winning ticket.

"You've done it," a general had said, standing next to Sergeant Blimes that day at the orphanage. "Where are your parents, so that we might welcome you to the program?"

"Sir," Sergeant Blimes had said, leaning over to whisper in his ear, "this is an orphanage. So..."

"Oh." The ambassador frowned, clearly confused. He looked every bit the part of the rich ambassador who had never even considered a world where anyone might want for food or money. To think that a kid might not have parents? Not a chance that had ever entered his mind.

Needless to say, Patrick had been quite relieved when Sergeant Blimes had taken him aside and said, "Listen, kid. You entered the program for a spot, but you don't have to accept. If you do, you get to play fulltime while en route during Sim-Sleep. It's sort of a... next-level step, you know? Like a placement exam."

Patrick had liked the sound of that and signed immediately, not even for a second doubting the decision.

He had only one question. "Once I arrive up there, do I have to stop playing?"

The sergeant had laughed. "Up there, Patrick, the whole world is essentially like this game world. All you do is play the game."

That was both a terrifying and exhilarating thought, but Patrick was already committed. He wasn't going to back down now. The sergeant led him into the ship, where they joined a group of other winners and then took the elevator up to their boarding dock. All moved in without saying a word, clearly unable to believe this was happening. What kid didn't dream of going to space? Even better, going to space while playing an intense video game? Getting to effectively *live* in the video game. It was exciting, but also incredibly nerve wracking. Not that he wasn't ready.

"You've been building up your characters for quite a while now, right?" Sergeant Blimes asked the group. They all nodded or mumbled that they had. He motioned them to a series of pods, the group leading up to the number four hundred. "Well there you go, then. You all likely have more experience than I do. You'll be naturals."

Patrick found his pod, number 399, and grinned. This was it. No more orphanages, no more people telling him what to do. From now on he would cut trees and slay zombies. Nothing else would matter until the moment they arrived on the planet. He stepped into the pod and sat, waiting as the sergeant closed the lids on the others, moving his direction. For one brief instant, he wondered if anyone on Earth would miss him, then laughed. Nope, and that didn't bother him one bit. He was going to live on Planet Gimli.

"Bye-bye, jerks," he muttered to himself and chuckled.

He glanced over at the others and noticed a girl, maybe a year or two younger, standing at the entrance to the pod bridge. She tucked her short hair behind her ear, eyed the room with wide eyes, and then noticed him looking.

Quickly averting his gaze, Patrick leaned back into his pod, closing his eyes as the sergeant lowered the lid of the pod to initiate the simulation.

[Grab Game Spaced on Amazon]

Made in the USA
Monee, IL
13 April 2022

94703317R00085